"This is wr[ong]

The finality of her words must have gotten through to Wade. He didn't try to kiss her again. "How?" he asked bitterly. "How could it be wrong?"

Kathryn clung to the sink for support. "We're family, for heaven's sake!"

"Only in the sense that when my father married your sister, we all came together as a unit. We've been over this ground before. You and I have no blood ties!"

Her face crimsoned. "So that makes it all right for us to carry on a tawdry affair behind their backs? Behind your *fiancée's?* I'm amazed you could even consider it!"

He didn't answer immediately, but something profound and painful was going on inside him, turning his eyes the dark green of an angry ocean. Unexpectedly, he moved away. "If you're ready," he said quietly, "I'll take you home."

Rebecca Winters, an American writer and mother of four, is a graduate of the University of Utah, who has also studied at schools in Switzerland and France, including the Sorbonne. She is currently teaching French and Spanish to junior high school students. Despite her busy schedule, Rebecca always finds time to write. She's already researching the background for her next Harlequin Romance!

Books by Rebecca Winters

MEANT FOR
EACH OTHER
Rebecca Winters

Harlequin Books

TORONTO • NEW YORK • LONDON
AMSTERDAM • PARIS • SYDNEY • HAMBURG
STOCKHOLM • ATHENS • TOKYO • MILAN
MADRID • WARSAW • BUDAPEST • AUCKLAND

ISBN 0-373-03228-5

Harlequin Romance first edition October 1992

MEANT FOR EACH OTHER

CHAPTER ONE

As THE PLANE circled the sunbaked Salt Lake Valley in preparation for landing, Kathryn Lawson's slender fingers tightened on the armrests. Her sister, Alice, would be waiting to take her home to Afton, the small Wyoming town where they'd been born and raised.

After their mother's death, Kathryn had moved in with Alice who, by that time, was married to Clyde Matheson, a widower, and owner of the general store in Afton. He had one son, and later on, two more children were born. They all lived happily in a tiny old house that Alice declared would always be home to Kathryn.

When Kathryn reached college age, she'd used her small inheritance from the sale of their parents' home to attend university in Boulder, Colorado. During that period she made visits to Afton at every opportunity. But when she went on to graduate school in San Diego, California, and married Philip, the visits stopped. In fact, she hadn't been back to Afton in five years. Yet she wasn't sure she'd done the right thing in coming now. She'd finally given in to Alice, who insisted that Kathryn needed to relax with her family for a while after the divorce.

Unfortunately Alice had become extremely protective since Kathryn's miscarriage and subsequent separation from Philip. Now that Kathryn had severed all ties with her ex-husband and had resigned from her teaching position at UCLA, Alice wouldn't leave her alone. She practically demanded that Kathryn come home for a month before she made any serious decisions about the rest of her life.

The screech of the wheels against the tarmac jarred Kathryn back to the present. When the plane had taxied to a full stop, she unfastened her seat belt and jumped up nervously to reach for her purse and overnight bag. She was aware of an uneasiness in the pit of her stomach, a sensation that owed nothing to the uneventful flight from San Diego to Salt Lake.

Since the trip was short—only an hour and a half—she still felt reasonably fresh in her white cotton suit with the tailored navy-and-white striped blouse beneath. It was the kind of outfit she wore when she lectured, to distinguish herself from the students who showed up for class in casual gear such as cutoffs and blue jeans.

She wore it now because to some extent it hid her recent weight loss. Kathryn's figure was normally well-rounded, but following her miscarriage and divorce, she hadn't been able to put on weight, a fact Alice would notice immediately.

She hoped her golden tan and rose-tinted sunglasses would hide the fatigue lines beneath her heavily lashed dark blue eyes. With her white high-heeled sandals, and her shoulder-length brown hair caught in a knot on top of her head, she knew she looked taller than her medium height and hoped her appearance gave the air of a confident thirty-year-old college teacher. The last thing she wanted was for Alice or Clyde to find out she was a mass of nerves.

Taking a fortifying breath, she walked off the plane and rode the escalator to the baggage-claim area on the main floor. Except for the contents of a large suit-case, and her overnight bag, all her things were in storage and would be sent on when she had a perma-nent address. Her old Toyota had been on its last legs when she left San Diego, so she'd sold it, planning to buy a new car at the first opportunity.

While she waited for her suitcase to show up on the carousel, her gaze flitted from one face to another as she scanned the room for signs of her sister, whose hair and coloring were similar to her own. But Kath-ryn was several inches taller and at one time had a more voluptuous figure; Alice, only five foot three, had a trim shape that made her look almost as youth-ful at forty as she had at twenty. Clyde, on the other hand, was a huskily built man over six feet tall, with light blond hair. Kathryn had always thought the two of them made an attractive couple.

As she stepped outside the entrance, the ninety-five-degree heat of the desert enveloped her. While other passengers found rides and climbed into the backs of taxis and limousines, she searched for Clyde's Dodge, then checked her watch again. Alice knew the plane was due at 5 p.m. Maybe she'd had car trouble. Anything could have happened on her way down from Afton.

At first Kathryn was too intent on watching for her sister to pay much attention to the truck pulling a horse trailer that glided to a stop at the curb. Then a tall dark-blond man levered himself from the cab. There was something familiar about him as he strode toward her, drawing her interest.

She couldn't help but admire the sinuous way his lean body moved, and the fit of scruffy-looking jeans molded to hips and powerful thighs like a second skin. His chest filled out a white T-shirt that had seen better days, yet the state of his clothes meant nothing in the face of such unconscious sexuality.

When he was a few feet away, Kathryn suddenly panicked. But it was too late, because he'd already plucked the sunglasses from her face, and she found herself the object of Wade Matheson's scrutiny.

Shocked by his presence, she couldn't say a word. She merely stared helplessly into the hazel eyes she'd always found so fascinating. In certain lights they seemed to take on different colors, from muted brownish green to tawny yellow. Right now they gleamed with a penetrating hostility that made her shiver.

Discomfited, she quickly shifted her gaze to his hair, once as fair as his father's. Five years had not only darkened it, but had added lines around his wide mouth, which now displayed an unmistakable hardness. More lines grooved his deeply tanned forehead, where several tendrils of hair clung to the heat-dampened skin. The uncompromising set of his straight nose and rugged features banished once and for all her memory of a twenty-year old boy, Clyde's son by his first wife. Why had she ever thought him so vulnerable?

For a moment, her mind flashed back to a time when she and Philip had been in Florence, Italy, admiring the works of Michelangelo. She could still remember seeing some of the famous sculptor's unfinished pieces. The figures were emerging from the stone, not complete but substantial enough to suggest the finished masterpiece.

That was how Wade had affected her then. Now, a man, not a boy, had walked away from the stone, complete and whole, and more attractive than she had dared to remember. Her eyes closed involuntarily to shut him out. Swaying slightly, she felt a firm hand grasp her elbow. His touch unnerved her and she jerked her arm away.

His eyes narrowed. "I'm beginning to understand what Allie meant when she said you needed a break."

Allie? Kathryn repeated the word to herself. In the past, Wade had always referred to Alice as Mom. His use of a nickname made Kathryn realize how much he had changed, how much everything had changed.

"What there is left of you looks as if the slightest breeze might blow you away."

Stung by his brutally honest assessment, she swallowed hard to regain her composure. She couldn't let him know how his unexpected presence had made chaos not only of her emotions, but of her carefully constructed plans to avoid him. "W-where's Alice?"

"At home getting things ready for you."

"When we spoke on the phone this morning, she said *she'd* meet me. I don't understand."

He folded his arms loosely across his chest. "What's to understand? I had to come to Salt Lake to buy a new quarter horse, so I volunteered to collect you."

"I see." She smoothed an imaginary strand of hair away from her temple. Naturally Alice would find nothing wrong in Wade's offer to pick up another member of the family. Perhaps she'd even encouraged it, since Wade had never come with the others to visit Kathryn in California.

Apparently he'd chosen to go to school each summer, instead; now at the age of twenty-five he'd already received his MBA and had established his own business. He'd always been more serious than his half brother and sister and infinitely more mature. According to Alice he was working night and day at his ranch and the family saw very little of him. As for Laurel and John, they were home from Wyoming State University for the summer, helping out at their dad's store to earn extra money. They'd assured Kathryn in a recent phone call that they were looking forward to seeing their one and only aunt.

"I doubt you 'see' at all." Wade's mocking tone came as a surprise.

"W-what do you mean?" Unwittingly she glanced at him, then realized her mistake as she confronted the anger smoldering in his eyes.

"Damn you, Kathryn. It's been five years. More like a lifetime. That's how long I've hated you."

The emotion in his voice, more than the words, brought unexpected pain. "Then—"

"Why am I here?" he broke in tersely, preventing her from finishing the question foremost on her mind. "You may well ask," he said in a low harsh tone. "When the folks told me you had actually deigned to honor the family with your presence, I decided our first meeting had better take place without an audience. After all, they're anticipating a joyous family reunion, and we wouldn't want to disappoint them, would we?"

With pounding heart, Kathryn looked around, aware that the intensity of their conversation was attracting the attention of several older couples standing nearby. "I don't think this is the place to be conducting the kind of discussion you have in mind," she said quietly, attempting to downplay a volatile situation.

"I agree. Let's go." Still holding her sunglasses, he picked up the suitcase with one hand, then gripped her upper arm firmly with the other. He ushered her between cars and limos toward the Ford pickup. Kathryn almost had to run to keep up with him, which was difficult in her heels.

Both the truck and trailer looked new. Despite her inner turmoil, part of her was still trying to deal with the fact that Wade had become so independent and successful since the last time they'd been together. But she didn't dare talk to him about anything that personal now. She found it hard to believe they had once communicated freely about everything, often sharing similar thoughts and attitudes on a variety of subjects.

Ever since childhood, Wade had talked about his dreams of owning and operating a dude ranch. Judging by Alice's reports, Wade's dream was fast becoming a reality.

After disposing of her suitcase and overnight bag in the back of the truck, he opened the passenger door for her. The high step forced her to stretch, causing her skirt to ride up above her knees, exposing her slender golden legs to his gaze. But if he was disturbed by the sight, she saw no evidence of it in his taut expression as he slammed the door and went around to the driver's side of the truck.

Tossing her sunglasses onto the dashboard, he slid behind the wheel and shut the door, enclosing them in an intimacy she had sought to avoid all these years. Apparently some habits never changed; in the sun-heated interior she could detect the clean fragrance of his shampoo. She'd always loved that scent. . . .

After such a long time of not seeing or talking to Wade, it disgusted her that his nearness still had the power to destroy her peace of mind and make her palms go clammy with tension. What had happened before she left for San Diego ought to have been forgotten, or at least buried deep in her subconscious, never to resurface. As long as she stayed in California, she'd managed not to dwell on the last summer she and Wade had spent together—when their friendship had changed into something else.

For years, shame had consumed her—shame that at the supposedly mature age of twenty-five, she could have found herself in an emotional entanglement with a twenty-year-old boy. Her last memory was of the two of them lying on his bed, wrapped in each other's arms, kissing and loving until she never wanted to stop.

Despite their age difference, Kathryn couldn't remember a time when she hadn't been drawn to him. After he'd graduated from high school and had started working at the store with his father to save money for college, she discovered that she preferred his company to almost anyone else's, even her boyfriends'.

But all that was over long ago, and she realized she couldn't avoid a reunion with her sister's family indefinitely, or Alice and Clyde would start prying into the reasons. Kathryn shuddered whenever she imagined their reaction if they'd ever found out what she and Wade had done while the rest of the family was on vacation in Banff, in the Canadian Rockies. But fortunately time and distance had negated that possibility.

When she realized where her thoughts had wandered, she gave herself a mental shake and stared out the window at the scorched foothills on her right. They'd left the airport and were headed north on I-15, trapped by a blistering sun that wouldn't set until much later. Its reflection glinted off the Great Salt Lake to the west, making Kathryn squint against the brightness.

She wanted to put on her sunglasses but she was worried that Wade might interpret it—correctly—as a desire to hide from him, to escape. She might as well have been sitting next to a stranger, albeit one who had just admitted he despised her. An involuntary shudder racked her body, something Wade was quick to notice.

"If the air-conditioning is too cold, I'll turn it down."

"Actually it feels good," she murmured, wishing he wasn't so observant. But then, it was one of the qualities that had made him such an appealing personality. Even at a young age, he was popular with everyone, particularly girls, who found his mind every bit as intriguing as his looks. Certainly, Kathryn hadn't been immune.

When she left for San Diego without saying goodbye to him, she had no doubt that she'd wounded his pride irreparably. But what choice had there been? If she'd stayed one more day alone in the house with him, she would have lost what little control she still had. After all, she was the adult, and it was up to her to avoid disaster. She willingly took the blame for a situation she should have been able to handle at the time, but didn't. Couldn't.

She spent the first year of self-imposed exile in San Diego hating herself for ever allowing her emotions to get the best of her. Once married, she'd finally managed to see the experience for what it was and could do nothing more than put it behind her, praying Wade had done the same.

But now it seemed that, given the opportunity, Wade wanted her to know there had been consequences to pay. As if she wasn't already aware that what they'd done had caused a permanent rift in the family!

As soon as Kathryn had gone to California, she learned from Alice that Wade had suddenly quit his job at the store, moved out of the house and gone to Fort Collins, Colorado, where he worked and went to college. Though Clyde hadn't actually said as much, Alice confided to Kathryn that her husband was hurt by Wade's decision to go to Colorado State instead of the University of Utah, which was much closer to Afton. Wade couldn't have made it plainer that he was striking out on his own.

His actions seemed to have a domino effect. John proceeded to inform the family that he wasn't spending the rest of his life in Afton. Now twenty, he was hoping to go to law school and dreamed of one day working as a corporate attorney in a big-city law firm. Nineteen-year-old Laurel planned to combine work and travel. Though Alice and Clyde had accepted the fact that their children wanted to pursue new vistas, Kathryn suffered pangs of guilt, because she felt that indirectly her relationship with Wade had altered the course of everyone's lives.

Growing more and more uncomfortable as the miles passed without a word from Wade, she finally broke the awkward silence, deciding it would be vastly safer to question him about his present plans.

"Alice tells me you're engaged," she said.

"Which couldn't possibly be of any interest to you, so we won't talk about it."

At his caustic remark, her hand almost snapped the chain on her purse. "For your information, this was not a situation I precipitated." Her voice shook with indignation. "If I'd had any idea you'd be picking me up at the airport, I would never have come."

"Exactly why I chose to take matters into my own hands."

She swallowed a retort. "Now that you've accomplished your objective, I can see no point in dragging this out any further. Let me off in Logan and I'll take a bus the rest of the way."

They were cresting the summit of Sardine Canyon; shifting gears, he shot her a menacing glance. "Obviously you feel no compunction about hurting the family even more than you already have."

"How dare you say that to me!"

"It's the truth," he said, seemingly unperturbed, his apparent disregard for her feelings infuriating her all the more. The Wade she'd once known would never have been so cruel. "They've accepted your flimsy excuses for staying away all these years, but that doesn't mean they've been happy about it. I, for one, would like to spare them any additional pain."

"I don't know what you're talking about." She tried to sound calm but failed miserably.

"Don't patronize me, Kathryn. It never worked in the past, and it won't work now. The fact is you never once visited Afton with your husband. Perhaps it hasn't occurred to you that Dad felt maybe his humble home and his lack of a college education wasn't good enough for you and your professor with his fancy beach house and his trail of impressive degrees."

"You're crazy!" she almost shouted at him. What he was saying now made a horrible kind of sense when viewed from Clyde's perspective, but nothing could have been further from the truth. Kathryn hadn't wanted the family to see how her marriage had failed. And more than that, she couldn't bear the thought of facing Wade, because she'd never satisfactorily resolved the issue of her attraction to him.

When the family came to the beach for a week's vacation each summer, it was easy enough for her and Philip to put on a good front, since there were so many activities to keep them all busy. But bringing Philip to

Afton would have been a mistake she would have regretted in too many ways to even consider.

"Hit a nerve, did I?" Wade taunted as he slowed to make a turn onto a side road, which led to a rustic inn noted for its succulent roast beef. She had been here with Wade on several occasions in the past, and she didn't want to be reminded of those times when their awareness of each other had made her forget common sense and propriety.

His unexpected action confused her, so that instead of answering with a scornful comment of her own, she said, "Why are we stopping?"

He turned off the ignition and opened his door, allowing the wildflower-scented breeze to fill the cab. "Perhaps you had dinner on the plane, but I haven't eaten since breakfast. Besides which, my horse needs exercise. If you'll go inside and order some sandwiches, I'll be along shortly to pay for them."

Arrogance never used to be part of the self-confidence she'd always associated with Wade. The years seemed to have changed him into someone harder and much more remote.

"I'm not hungry, so I'll walk your horse while you buy something to tide you over. That way we can get to Afton sooner."

With a grimace, he subjected her to another thorough appraisal, one that made her strangely uncomfortable. "You look as if you haven't had a proper meal in days," he said flatly, not bothering to acknowledge her offer.

"I'm sorry if my appearance displeases you." As soon as the words left her mouth she realized her mistake. She was letting Wade get to her, responding to his gibes when she ought to ignore them.

"Did I say that?" he lashed out.

Trying not to let his abrasive manner fluster her, she said, "Wade, I don't know what you hoped to accomplish by picking me up, but now that you've had your say, let's go home. It's been a long day."

"Tell me about it," he said in an oddly hoarse voice, his eyes intent on her face. "But just so we understand each other, Allie and Dad expect things to be the way they used to be. You and I both know that's impossible, but for their sake we're going to arrive at the house and pretend. We're going to act as though we like each other—even if the idea is repulsive. And if you had any thoughts about only staying for a few days, you can forget them."

His assessment of the situation astounded her so much that she was slow to understand. "I—I'm not sure what you mean."

After a long pause he said, "The folks have plans for you that involve more than a weekend visit. Provided you're willing, of course."

"What plans?" she whispered, still reeling from the effect of his words.

"Since it's their idea, I'll leave it to them to explain." Whatever he knew, it sounded as if he liked the prospect even less than she did.

"I—I'm not exactly sure of my plans except that I'm going to see about a teaching job, preferably in Colorado."

Much as she enjoyed the ocean, Kathryn had always disliked the crowds and jammed freeways of California, and she missed the mountains, particularly the Tetons. She actually craved the relaxed casual pace of a Western college town like Fort Collins or Boulder, where she'd gone to undergraduate school. If she secured a teaching position at either university, she would spend the rest of the summer finding a condo to decorate and getting herself settled before the fall term started.

"If you care at all for the family's feelings, I suggest you keep your future plans to yourself. For tonight, anyway," he added in a warning voice.

Flashing her another distinctly hostile glance, he got out of the truck and slammed the door. A few minutes later she could feel the vibration of hooves as Wade led his horse from the trailer, leaving her to her own tortured thoughts.

She should have heeded the foreboding that told her not to let Alice pressure her into this visit. Already Wade's physical presence was having an alarming effect on her senses, despite the years of separation. How could she stay longer than a weekend with him around? Yet how could she leave so abruptly after what he'd told her about Alice's plans?

I was a fool to come back, she cried inwardly, hiding her face in her hands. Wade had placed her in an impossible position.

On the plane from San Diego to Salt Lake, Kathryn had felt a hundred years older and wiser. And she'd reasoned that now Wade had grown up, he, too, had finally put aside what had happened in the past, relegating it to proximity and an excess of hormones.

Knowing he had a fiancée and that he'd only be an occasional visitor to the house had convinced Kathryn it was possible for her to accept Alice's invitation. But nothing had turned out the way she'd imagined. *Whatever had possessed her?*

CHAPTER TWO

"I THOUGHT YOU WANTED to eat," she commented when Wade returned to the truck only a few minutes later.

"I thought so, too," came the oblique reply as he inserted the key into the ignition and flicked on the radio to an all-news station. The broadcast prevented further conversation while they drove the last hour and a half to Afton. But even if World War III had been announced, Kathryn wouldn't have heard a word. She was far too aware of Wade's nearness, the way his well-honed body maneuvered the truck with practiced ease.

She found herself wondering about his fiancée. Were they deeply in love? How long had they been seeing each other? Was their relationship an intimate one? Unconsciously she tightened her fingers on the chain of her handbag.

"Kathryn?"

She jerked her head around guiltily, astonished to discover that he'd been talking to her. "What is it?"

"Good grief," he muttered, "you're as jumpy as a cat! In case it escaped your notice, we're home."

Sure enough, she could see the little red two-story brick house with its beckoning white shutters as Wade pulled to a stop at the end of the long driveway. The rows of poplars that lined it created a sensation of peace and order, a complete contrast to her thoughts. Kathryn had been so preoccupied she hadn't even noticed the sign indicating that they had entered Afton. It was one of several hamlets in the Star Valley area, which was famous for its dairy herds and Swiss cheese.

"No matter what your personal feelings are, we'll present a united front to the family. Agreed?" he demanded harshly. "That means hiding the revulsion you feel toward me."

Revulsion? she mouthed to herself. Did he honestly believe she hated him for what had happened in the past? She couldn't take it in.

"Welcome home!" Alice cried in delight as she flung open the passenger door. The commotion prevented Kathryn from responding to Wade's faulty interpretation of her actions.

"Alice, Clyde," she said in a strained voice as she climbed down from the truck and hugged them both. Laurel, dark and petite like her mother, stood a little behind her parents, waiting impatiently to embrace Kathryn.

While Wade walked back to the trailer to tend to his horse, John came out of the house and caught her in a bear hug. He, too, was dark-haired like Alice, and though not as tall as his father, his body was well-defined from lifting weights. He had a conventionally handsome face that attracted a fair share of admirers.

But it was Wade who exuded such potent male sexuality that few women were immune. Kathryn had never met another man like him, and she blamed her lack of response not only to Philip but to all the other male acquaintances in her life on her dangerous attraction to him.

Steeling herself not to look at Wade, she gave the family her full attention while they helped take her things into the house. The second she stepped inside the cozy living room with its early-American decor, Kathryn detected the wonderful aroma of barbecued spareribs and homemade rolls. Everything looked exactly the same as it had five years ago, and it was suddenly hard to remember she'd ever been away.

"While you freshen up, Laurel and I will put the food on the table," Alice told her. "We had a snack earlier, but didn't want to eat a big meal until you came, and frankly we're starving." She raised dark eyebrows, which met her bangs. "So, hurry, okay?"

Kathryn gave her sister another hug. "I'm starving, too," she lied. "I'll be as fast as I can."

"I put you in Wade's old room," Alice said to Kathryn, who had reached the staircase. "Today I cleaned it thoroughly and made the bed with clean sheets—and a new quilt I sewed for you. I hope you'll be comfortable."

Eyeing her older sister with affection, Kathryn murmured, "You know I will. In fact, I've always loved this house, because you've made it the ultimate home. No wonder Clyde's crazy about you. But remember, I'm family, not a guest, and I'll do my share of the work while I'm here." *Which won't be for very long,* Kathryn promised herself as she dashed up the steep narrow staircase to the second floor.

Two bedrooms adjoined a small bathroom at the head of the stairs, where the hall was lined with family photographs. Wade's room was the attic, a cleverly renovated area reached by yet another, even steeper flight of stairs. She approached it with pounding heart, trying desperately not to remember what had happened in this room the last time she'd been in it with Wade.

A dresser and wardrobe stood against one wall, the same as before. With the exception of a framed photo of a ten-year-old Wade holding up a huge trout as he sat in a rowboat next to his father, all the familiar mementos and pictures were gone.

On the other wall was his old bed, and above it a round window. Despite the deepening shadows, she could see the fertile Swisslike countryside stretching far into the distance.

As she crossed the threshold, she immediately caught sight of the beautiful new patchwork quilt. Alice had pieced together hundreds of colorful fabric scraps in a traditional wedding-ring pattern. Kathryn recognized many of the prints from dresses she and Alice and their mother used to wear. There were even a few pieces cut from some of her dad's old neckties.

A rush of heartwarming memories flooded her mind. Her eyes misted as she stepped past her bags to examine the perfect stitches, reflecting on the hundreds of hours it must have taken Alice to make the quilt.

"It's gorgeous," she whispered to herself, hugging a corner of it to her chest, unable to handle so much emotion at one time.

"Allie worked on it day and night." The deep voice reached her ears at the same moment that her sunglasses landed on top of the quilt. Kathryn spun around to see Wade lounging against the doorjamb, gazing at her thoughtfully. "It's her welcome-home present."

Kathryn's mouth went dry at the sight of his solid frame so close to hers, dwarfing the dimensions of the little room, haunting her with memories. "It's the most beautiful gift I've ever received in my life, but I couldn't possibly keep it. Alice made it and it belongs to her."

Frown lines marred his features and he straightened. "Last year she quilted a similar one for herself. She'd be crushed if you didn't accept it."

Kathryn had no reason not to believe him, but his proximity prevented her from thinking, let alone making conversation. Perhaps now that Wade was engaged, it didn't bother him to be alone with her in his old room. But Kathryn didn't think she could cope with the situation much longer.

She smoothed the quilt back into place. "Please tell Alice I'll be right down."

He stayed where he was, his legs casually crossed at the ankles, and raked her with a probing gaze. "You're pale under that tan. If you don't feel up to eating with the family tonight, we can bring dinner to you."

"I'm fine. A little tired, but surely that's natural."

His mouth tightened in displeasure. "There's nothing natural about the bags under your eyes or the way your clothes hang on you. From what I've heard, divorce is supposed to be something positive, fix what's wrong. But I suppose it depends on who asked for the divorce, and as I understand it, that was Philip. Are you so much in love with your ex-husband you've stopped living?"

She took a steadying breath to fight the shame she felt whenever she thought of how she'd failed Philip. He had been a charming bachelor who'd chaired her doctoral dissertation at UCLA and had pursued her from the moment she arrived in San Diego. But with hindsight, she knew she would never have said yes to his proposal if she hadn't been so guilt-ridden over Wade. "I'd rather not discuss it."

"Maybe you should. A twenty-pound weight loss hasn't done you much good."

"Fifteen," she corrected him. "Sometimes miscarriages affect women that way." *Not to mention a disintegrating marriage.* Philip had been so decent about everything it had made the situation that much more devastating for Kathryn.

A bleak look entered Wade's eyes. "I'm sorry you lost your baby, Kathryn, but more than ever you need to take care of yourself."

She bestowed a false smile on him. "I'm stronger than I look. Besides, being thin is fashionable."

"For a model, perhaps," he said, his lips twisting unpleasantly. Kathryn turned away from his assessing eyes, unaccountably hurt by his censure. But maybe that was because there had been a time when he had told her, shown her, how beautiful she was to him, and her feminine pride wanted him to retain that image.

"I need to wash before we eat."

"Be my guest." He stood aside with his hands on his hips while she brushed past him. The slight contact made her senses come alive, and she hurried down the stairs to the bathroom where she could lock herself in and be alone with her chaotic thoughts.

But she couldn't stay in there indefinitely, not with everyone waiting for her, anxious to catch up on months of news. And though she knew the family wouldn't bring up the divorce or anything to do with Philip, Wade would be watching her from across the table, listening to every word she said, analyzing her responses with that keen intelligence of his.

After rinsing her face and hands, she applied more blusher and lipstick, then arranged her hair in an attempt to look in control, if nothing else.

When she walked into the kitchen a few minutes later, the family was already seated at the square wooden table. Alice had placed a bowl of wildflowers in the center and the effect was lovely.

A beaming Clyde stood up and pulled out a chair, indicating she should sit between him and Alice. When she took her place, he gazed around at each of them with a suspicious brightness in the hazel eyes so like his son's. Twice he had to clear his throat before he could begin, and all the while she could feel Wade's inscrutable glances.

"Kathryn," Clyde said, "I guess I don't have to tell you how thrilled I am to see this family together again. You've been missed, by your sister and me, your niece and your nephew. Now, let's give thanks."

After the blessing, Kathryn expressed her happiness at being under their roof once more, then grasped her sister's hand and started to thank her for the quilt. But too many feelings were erupting, and she burst in to tears.

Alice smiled, obviously touched by such a genuine display of emotion. "I told you that one day I'd do something with our old dresses."

After a minute Kathryn pulled herself together. "It's a gift I'll cherish all my life. I wish there was another way to thank you besides saying those two simple words."

"Maybe there is." Clyde winked mysteriously, reminding her of the conversation with Wade, and her heart sank. "But let's eat first."

Everyone concurred, and for a little while the talk consisted mostly of requests to pass the ribs and the scalloped potatoes, interspersed with questions from Laurel about life at the beach, a topic she seemed to find endlessly fascinating. Wade remained aloof, though from time to time he stared broodingly at Kathryn, who did everything in her power to act as natural as possible.

She chatted with her niece and nephew about their studies and managed to ply Clyde with dozens of questions about his business, which appeared to be thriving. This went on until the hot apple pie with rich cream and cheese slices was served. At this point everyone praised Alice for the terrific meal, and silence reigned until dessert had been eaten.

"Shall we tell her now?" Clyde whispered to his wife, but Kathryn couldn't help overhearing.

"Tell me what, Clyde?" She chuckled in spite of her nervousness about what was coming. "You're obviously bursting with something important to say. I'm all ears."

His grin encompassed the entire family. "Well," he drawled, "if it meets with your approval, we're going on vacation tomorrow. All of us. For three whole days we won't do anything but lie around, fish a little and eat as much as we want."

Kathryn panicked. When he said *all*, he meant Wade, too. "I don't understand. I thought July and August were your busiest months and you couldn't afford to take time off for a trip."

He made a gesture that told her not to worry. "You remember Jack Burns?"

"The police chief's son?"

"That's right. Well, he's started working for me part-time, and he does a good job when I want to take time off." A tender expression appeared on his face. "Now that we've got you home, we're not going to waste a single minute. Of course—" he broke off to exchange glances with Alice "—if you'd rather have privacy and not go anywhere for a while, we understand. You can have the house to yourself for a few days."

Kathryn wouldn't have dared disappoint Clyde; she didn't need the rapier-sharp reminder coming from Wade's eyes, telling her to go along with this, or else. "Of course I want to vacation with you. Where are we going?" she asked in a quiet voice.

"Elk Island!" Laurel cried with her usual enthusiasm.

It was what she'd feared. Elk Island had to be the most wonderful place on earth, as far as Kathryn was concerned. But too many memories of Wade and other family outings were connected with it. The island, which boasted no bears and few campsites, could only be reached by boat, and you had to obtain a permit from the park service months ahead of time to camp there. It rose out of Jackson Lake, the clearest and bluest of lakes, with the Teton Mountains towering overhead like giant sentinels. Much as she loved the place, she didn't know how she'd be able to stand going there again. But it seemed she had no choice.

"Wade's bringing the parasail and the kayaks," Laurel was explaining. "And I've got a new three-person spring-bar tent I bought in Cheyenne. You can bed down with me, Aunt Kathryn."

"I have a dome tent Kathryn can use." This from Wade, who knew better than anyone the battle going on inside her. "Assuming you might like your privacy."

"Then it's settled," Alice announced as she began clearing the table.

"Will your fiancée be joining us?" Kathryn asked in a deceptively calm voice, hoping she sounded interested without making it obvious that she was consumed with curiosity about the woman he'd chosen to marry.

"Not this time, I'm afraid," Wade answered in even tones so that she couldn't tell how he really felt about his fiancée's absence.

"Amy's in Florida showing horses and won't be back for a few more days," John supplied moodily, diverting Kathryn's attention. "Her family raises quarter horses on their property near the mouth of Alta Canyon in Salt Lake."

Kathryn's glance darted back to Wade, who remained silent, eyeing his brother speculatively. She realized Wade had probably gone to his fiancée's ranch that morning to pick up his horse. A strange pain twisted her heart at the knowledge that this Amy was already so intimately involved with the family. Evidently she had won everyone's approval, particularly John's, which was no small feat, since from adolescence he had considered himself a connoisseur of women.

"How did you meet her?" Kathryn asked Wade before she could think twice about it.

"They met at a horse show in the Salt Palace. She's a fabulous rider."

Once again John had spoken for Wade. If she didn't know better, she would have thought *John* was engaged to Amy.

"And her family is loaded!"

"Laurel!" Alice stopped scraping dishes at the sink to reprimand her daughter. "Enough of that talk!"

"It's all right, Allie," Wade said, studying Kathryn while he finished a second piece of pie. "One day, when Laurel's a little older and more experienced, she'll understand that men—and women—who equate the size of a bank account with something as intangible as love have questionable principles."

Kathryn had the uncomfortable feeling that Wade wasn't referring to Laurel at all, and she sat straighter in her chair. Surely he didn't think she, Kathryn, had married Philip because *he* had money....

Anxious to change the subject, she switched her attention to John, whose behavior was peculiar, to say the least. "Is there a special girl in your life right now?"

"Could be."

"You sound positively mysterious," Kathryn teased, attempting to humor him, because she sensed strange undercurrents here. And she certainly hadn't imagined the glance Laurel exchanged with her mother.

"But now you're back, I'd just as soon be on vacation with you," John spoke in shades of his former self. "Let's face it, you always did look better in a bathing suit than any other female on the beach, and you're a lot more fun."

Now Kathryn *knew* something was wrong. "You're overdoing it, Johnny-boy."

Everyone laughed except Wade, whose features had remained impassive throughout the meal. Suddenly he pushed himself away from the table, announcing to no one in particular that he was going outside to finish loading the motorboat. John mumbled something about getting his wet suit to fix the tear in it, and Clyde followed Wade out the door.

Kathryn told herself she was glad of the respite. While Alice washed dishes, Kathryn dried them, turning her attention to her niece while she put the plates away in the cupboard. "How about you, Laurel? Alice tells me you've been dating a fraternity boy quite regularly."

"I have. But now he's working in Alaska for the summer, so I won't see him until fall."

"But just think about the letters you'll be getting all summer," Kathryn said, admiring her niece's small frame and pretty features.

"I hope," she murmured, communicating with gestures that she didn't want John, who had brought down his wet suit and was busy glueing a rip, to hear the details.

"Fix that outside please," Alice urged. "The fumes make me sick."

Grumbling softly, John did her bidding. When he'd gone out the back door, Alice looked at Kathryn over Laurel's head, and they both smiled in secret understanding. "Kathryn, it's getting late and I know you've had a long day. While everyone else is still busy down here, feel free to shower and go to bed. Clyde wants to leave by seven tomorrow morning."

"But what about all the food we usually make?" she asked as the phone rang. Laurel rushed to answer it.

"I've been cooking for days. Everything's packed and ready to go."

"You're sure?"

The older woman nodded. "You look dead on your feet."

"Wade said the same thing, so I must be a sight!" She darted her sister a wry grimace.

"If anything, you're even more beautiful than you used to be. Don't let what Wade says bother you. He's always been the type to notice everything, and in spite of the fact that he hasn't seen you in five years, he cares a great deal for you. That's why he picked you up today, so he could make up for lost time."

Kathryn moistened her lips nervously. "I have to admit I was surprised when he showed up at the airport, but it was ... good to see him again."

"I'm glad," Alice said, cocking her head pertly to the side. "For some strange reason, Clyde has this feeling you two weren't getting along before you left for San Diego, but I told him he was crazy."

"He is. Wade and I have always been friends," Kathryn assured her sister, but she wondered if Alice believed her. Clyde was a sensitive man. How much did he really know and understand about her relationship with Wade?

Judging by what Wade had told her during the drive to Afton, Clyde's concern stemmed from his worry that Kathryn didn't think his home was good enough for Philip. But Alice's comment put a totally different construction on things, one that hit too close to the mark.

Maybe it was Wade, and not his father, who believed Kathryn was a snob and didn't consider their home up to her husband's standards. That would make the most sense. Particularly since she suspected that Wade believed she'd married Philip for the material things he could give her.

The ironic part was that Philip didn't even have that much money. Yes, he was a professor who made a good salary, and because he was an only child, he'd inherited some money and the beach house from his parents. But he was by no means a wealthy man.

"If there's nothing more for me to do, I think I'll go upstairs. A shower sounds heavenly."

"Good." Alice continued to wipe off the counters. "I'll see you in the morning."

Kathryn couldn't resist hugging her sister goodnight. "Tell me something before I go. What's wrong with John? He seems different. Kind of sullen and moody."

"He is." Alice smoothed the bangs off her forehead. "The truth is I'm very much afraid he's fallen for Amy. It happened the first time Wade brought her to dinner."

"What?"

Alice would have said more, but just then Wade came in through the back door carrying an empty cooler. His eyes met Kathryn's. "I hope you're planning on an early night. You obviously need the rest. Think you'll be able to sleep?"

What did he mean by that? "Of course."

"Even without the sound of the surf?" One dark blond eyebrow lifted in question. Out of the corner of her eye she saw Alice stare at Wade with a puzzled expression on her face. For some reason Wade seemed intent on reminding her of her life with Philip, a fact he didn't bother to hide from Alice.

"Have you forgotten I was born and raised here in Afton? The peace and quiet of Star Valley are more conducive to sleep than any number of waves pounding against the sand. Good night, Wade, and thanks for picking me up at the airport."

After a long silence he said, "My pleasure. See you tomorrow."

She felt his eyes on her retreating back as she headed for the stairs off the living room. She ran up both flights and flung herself, breathless, into the attic bedroom. But instead of gathering the things for her shower, she opened the window in time to see Wade's truck and trailer pull away from the house and disappear down the highway. For the longest time she simply stood there, breathing in the scent of honeysuckle on the warm night air, filled with a gnawing emptiness she couldn't explain.

Not liking the mood she was in, she hurried down to the bathroom. She stood under the cool, cleansing spray, wondering how she was going to get through the next three days with Wade continually around. Her only consolation was that he, too, dreaded the prospect of spending so much time in her company and would do everything possible to avoid unnecessary contact.

While she dried herself, she could see her image reflected in the mirror. She used to worry about being too curvy, but now she was too thin and would look terrible in a two-piece bathing suit.

Since the moment Philip had told her it was no use, that he wanted a divorce, she had lost interest in a lot of things, because she realized she was to blame. From that point on she didn't give much thought to her physical appearance. No wonder Wade had reacted so strongly when he first saw her. She bore little resemblance to the woman who had run away from Afton and from him.

She pressed a hand against her flat stomach, scarcely able to believe she had once been five months pregnant. Oh, how she had wanted that baby, praying it would draw her and Philip closer together! But her wishes hadn't materialized. At least the doctors had convinced her that although this miscarriage was unavoidable, there was no reason she couldn't have a successful pregnancy in the future.

Since she'd been given a small taste of impending motherhood, she ached to become pregnant again and to actually give birth. But only if she was married to the right man—a man with whom she was deeply in love, a man she would always welcome into her heart and her bed. She had wanted that man to be Philip, had tried to be the perfect wife to him. But unlike her experience with Wade, the fire wasn't there, and in time she and Philip grew apart.

Rebuking herself for allowing thoughts of Wade to drift to such dangerous channels, she put on her nightgown and hurried upstairs. But as soon as she slid beneath the covers, she was painfully reminded of the night Wade had brought her to this room. She could still feel the way his mouth clung to hers.

And though everything about their relationship had been wrong, the passion he had aroused in her had been so overwhelming, she didn't know how she'd found the strength to pull away from him before it was too late. Even now she was haunted by his husky voice telling her he'd been in love with her forever. She shivered, remembering how he had pleaded with her to stay, how he had begged her to let him make love to her, claiming she wanted it, too—and he'd been right.

Every so often, she tortured herself wondering what would have happened if she *had* spent the night with him. In her heart of hearts, she knew they would never have been satisfied with one night. From the very beginning it seemed their lives had been on some kind of collision course, as if the change in their relationship, from affection to intimacy, was meant to be. Before she left for San Diego, the one thing—the only thing— that consumed either of them was the burning desire to make love. Surely a baby would have resulted. Their baby.

Kathryn lay there in a cold sweat. As soon as the trip to the Tetons was over, she would leave Afton. Not only because she couldn't take being around Wade any longer, but because she had no wish to meet his fiancée, the woman who had the right to receive his love and to be the mother of his children.

And later on, would meeting Amy as his wife make it any more palatable? a tiny voice in her head persisted in asking.

Kathryn already knew the answer to that question, and her thoughts drifted to John. If, as Alice suggested, he had fallen for Wade's fiancée, then Kathryn could well understand John's touchiness. She wondered why he chose to work in Afton all summer

where he ran the risk of seeing Wade and Amy together. *Maybe he couldn't help himself...*

But Kathryn couldn't bear the thought of seeing
Wade with another woman. And she had no intention
of putting herself through that particular torture. She
stifled her groans with the pillow.

CHAPTER THREE

CLYDE SAT AT THE WHEEL of his Dodge station wagon and looked over his shoulder. "Everybody ready?"

"We're all here and packed in like sardines," Laurel replied. Kathryn, who sat in the back between her and John with a stack of towels on her lap, was already feeling the heat. An outing to Elk Island meant they took everything but the kitchen sink. Even the motorboat, which was on a trailer attached to the car, had been filled to overflowing with camping equipment and supplies.

Clyde turned to Alice. "How about you, honey? Can you think of anything we forgot? Speak now, because I swear I'm not coming back."

"If we've forgotten something, it can't be important. Let's go. Wade will be wondering what happened to us."

A quick glance at her watch told Kathryn they were leaving an hour later than originally planned, but that was nothing new.

Once they were en route north, excitement lit Alice's face as she shifted in the front seat to talk to Kathryn. "You've never seen that piece of property Wade purchased for his ranch, have you?"

"No." And she didn't want to. The less involved she was with Wade, the better.

"Three years ago it was nothing but an unwanted parcel of land with a couple of broken-down old cabins. Since Wade took over the property, you wouldn't recognize it. Not only has he rebuilt the cabins, but he's put up two more, plus a barn, and he's working on his own house. Next summer he'll open the place for business."

Kathryn blinked. "Then how's he earning his living now?"

"Over the years, he's made some lucrative investments. And he's the accountant for several big companies in the area, including Elliott Lumber. They supply him with materials and labor in return for his services," Clyde explained. "Any spare time Wade finds, he spends fencing his land. The way he sees it, the river running through his property provides some of the best fly fishing in the world, and he figures that in no time at all, people will flock to his place."

That sounded like Wade, Kathryn mused to herself. He had more optimism, more confidence, than any person she'd ever known. He was also endowed with a steely determination that would take him wherever he wanted to go.

"He already has horses and camping gear for taking pack trips into the Tetons this fall," Alice continued, making no secret of her admiration for her stepson. "Pretty soon he'll be able to purchase rafts and trucks for white-water trips."

"Wade works so hard that Amy complains she never sees him," Laurel confided. "I can't say I blame her. If I were engaged, I'd be plenty upset if I was the one who always had to do the running."

Though she dreaded the answer, Kathryn couldn't help asking, "Have they set a date for their wedding?"

"No," John interjected quietly. "Not yet."

Alice hastened to fill in the unnatural silence that followed. "You know Wade. He won't marry her until he can support them with his own income, and since his money is all tied up right now, it could be a while."

For no logical reason, Kathryn felt a wave of relief spread through her body. "He's always wanted to run a dude ranch," she mused aloud. "In time I should imagine he'll be very successful."

"And that thrills you, doesn't it, darling?" Alice squeezed her husband's shoulder.

"I have to admit I'm pleased to know *one* of my three children will be around to visit their old man occasionally."

"Daddy!" Laurel was sitting behind her father and flung her arms about his neck. "I'll always come home for visits, no matter where I live. You know that," she said, kissing the top of his blond head.

"That's very reassuring, but once you're tied to a career, it isn't always that easy to get away, is it, Kathryn?"

She was saved from responding to Clyde's comment by Laurel's happy squeal. She'd spotted Wade in the distance and despite the air-conditioning had opened her window to wave madly.

Kathryn's gaze darted automatically to the white truck parked at the side of a dirt road next to the highway. She noticed a couple of kayaks in the back. "His ranch is about a mile from here," Alice said for Kathryn's benefit, pointing west. But Kathryn couldn't make out much more than flowering meadows and pines.

Clyde pulled off to the side of the highway and got out. Without conscious thought, Kathryn fastened her attention on Wade as he vaulted from his truck, dressed in old cutoffs, a T-shirt and loafers. Her stomach lurched with unfamiliar sensations as she watched the smooth movement of his lean coordinated body. He wasn't handsome in the conventional sense, but his wonderful bone structure, deeply tanned skin and medium-length dark blond hair gave him a compelling attractiveness. She watched, entranced, as the soft breeze disheveled his hair, and tendrils drifted across his brow.

Both men sauntered over to the driver's side of the station wagon. Wade leaned his head inside, took one look at Kathryn sandwiched between the other two and said, "Come on out, Kathryn. There's no sense getting squashed when I have an empty truck."

She shook her head frantically. "I'm fine right here. Really."

"Stop being diplomatic," Alice chided with a smile. "You'll be much more comfortable driving with Wade."

"Go on," Clyde urged, leaving Kathryn no choice but to comply. Once again fate had conspired against her.

"Thanks," Laurel whispered. "Now I can breathe."

John said absolutely nothing, but Kathryn didn't miss the strange stare he gave her and Wade before he got out of the car so she could slide across the seat.

Her ponytail bobbed as she walked around the front of the car and came face-to-face with Wade. She went cold then hot as she felt his penetrating gaze follow the outline of her body beneath a washed-out yellow T-shirt before dropping to her long tanned legs exposed by a pair of faded blue running shorts. White tennis shoes completed her outfit; unfashionable, she knew, but it couldn't be helped. She hadn't had time to do any shopping and nothing else in her wardrobe fit.

"Shall we go?" he murmured in a low deep voice that took her back five years.

With a sense of déjà vu she accepted his help and climbed into the cab of the truck. Maybe it was her imagination, but she thought she felt his fingers press briefly against the soft warm skin near her underarm before he released her to close the door.

And maybe she was losing her mind, because his grim expression was the first thing she noticed when he got in on the driver's side and started the engine.

Without saying a word, he followed Clyde's Dodge and trailer onto the highway and they drove for several miles before he so much as glanced at her.

"For your information, Dad said he wanted to have a little talk with John and suggested you ride with me."

"I see."

"I don't think so. According to the folks, John hasn't been the most pleasant person to be around lately."

Kathryn lowered her head, not anxious to pursue the subject any further, particularly since Alice had revealed the source of John's pain. "Growing up is never easy."

His harsh laugh surprised her. "Thus speaks the voice of experience."

"If you don't mind, I'd like to change the subject."

"So would I. Let's talk about your divorce."

Her throat practically closed up. "I'd rather not."

"That's why you're so tense, isn't it?" he observed with uncanny perception. "You're brittle as glass, Kathryn. One day you'll shatter if you keep the pain locked in."

"I'd prefer to talk about your fiancée," Kathryn countered. "What's she like?"

His jaw hardened. "For one thing, she's open. For another, she's honest, which is more than I can say for you."

Her fingernails dug into her palms. "She sounds like a paragon. Congratulations."

"Sarcasm doesn't become you," he answered so calmly she felt her blood pressure rise.

"Look, Wade. Maybe it's best we don't discuss our personal lives."

"I don't know how we can avoid it, but I'm willing to leave the matter alone for the moment. What's important is that we pretend to get along while we're on vacation. Your visit is vitally important to the family—in fact, that's why Dad's having his little talk with John. The others won't thank him if he's the reason you decide to leave again."

"I'm not sure what you're implying, but I'll only be in Afton for a short time, and John's behavior has nothing to do with anything."

"How short?" he demanded.

"As I told you last night, I have a career to think about," she exclaimed, linking her hands together.

"Career be damned. What if I told you the folks have hired a contractor to remodel the second floor of the store as an apartment for you?"

"What?"

"It's meant to be a surprise. I imagine they were going to tell you at the lake."

"But I couldn't possibly live here!"

"Why not? You used to tell me you loved Afton and would never want to live anyplace else."

"Wade, I was young when I said that. I didn't know anything about the world."

He swore softly. "Now you're sounding like John and Laurel. As if living here has somehow deprived or diminished you."

"You're twisting my words."

"Am I? Then you tell me what you really meant."

Heat seemed to blaze from her cheeks. "I'm a math teacher, for heaven's sake."

"So take a position in one of the high schools around here. The world is crying out for decent math teachers."

She grabbed at the first excuse she could think of. "The salary is hardly comparable to that of a university's."

"Surely your ex-husband pays you enough alimony to compensate for the drastic drop in your income."

Through clenched teeth she said, "You seem to have some inflated idea of Philip's financial status. Although it's none of your business, I've received all the alimony I'm going to get from him. I'm on my own now."

"Are you telling me the truth?" His eyes glittered dangerously.

"Why would I lie? We both wanted the divorce over and done with." In truth her conscience hadn't allowed her to take money from Philip once she'd left California. It wouldn't have been right, and she couldn't have lived with herself.

"What kind of man is he?" When she glanced at him, she saw a dull red flush stain his cheeks. She knew he only looked like that when he was truly angry.

"He was wonderful, if you must know."

There was a brief pause. "Then why did he divorce you?"

She turned her head to stare out her window. "Because I wasn't a good wife to him."

"Why not?"

"Not all women are cut out for marriage, like Alice."

"You're lying to me, because if that was the case he would have divorced you long ago. Were you unfaithful to him? Is that why he isn't willing to part with any more money?"

His assumption was so close to the truth she was speechless. She felt the blood drain from her face. "I think this line of questioning has gone far enough."

"The hell it has." He floored the accelerator. "So who was this man who got you to betray your marriage vows?"

"I already told you it's none of your business. How would you like it if I asked you something that intimate and personal, like how long you've been sleeping with your fiancée?"

"I didn't know you were so curious," he responded with a wry twist of his lips, "but if you really want to know, I'll tell you."

Kathryn was mortified by what she'd said and wished she could disappear. "I doubt your fiancée would appreciate the intimate details of your life being discussed with anyone else.''

"She'll never know."

"That's disgusting."

"Maybe, but then you and I have shared a rather unusual relationship, haven't we? As I recall, we used to be able to talk about anything—and we came close to sharing everything."

Her body shook so hard she was sure he could feel it. "That was a long time ago, when you were very young and I should have known better."

"I wondered when we'd get down to that. I have news for you, Kathryn. Our age difference never meant a damn thing and if you were honest, you'd admit I'm right."

"It made enough of a difference that I wouldn't take advantage of your youth and inexperience."

"I know in my gut that I could have persuaded you to sleep with me. And if I'd been concerned only with gratifying my own desires, I would have."

"That's where you're wrong, Wade." But her assertion sounded less than convincing; somehow she realized he was speaking the truth.

"Am I?" His questions had a way of getting under her skin, tearing down the fragile defenses she'd built around herself, the careful explanations she'd contrived. "Surely by now it's occurred to you that I allowed you to escape from my bed only because you weren't ready for a total commitment."

"T-that's not true."

"Isn't it? I was there, remember? And at that moment, the only thing we cared about was what we felt in each other's arms. Nothing else, including age, had any meaning."

"You're exaggerating what happened," she said, trying to dismiss the most significant moment in her life.

"If that's true, then I wonder why you ran off to San Diego the next day."

"Because it was time to go and I had plans for my life."

"And they were so important you left before Allie and Dad could get back from their trip to say goodbye? I hardly think so."

"You can believe what you want, Wade."

"Oh, I do. As far as I'm concerned, it was your damn guilt over getting involved with a family member—a *younger* family member—even though we're not actually related. You were supposed to be my *aunt* Kathryn, and that made our feelings for each other forbidden. So your guilt sent you flying and at some point you decided to hate me to ease it. And you've gone on hating me ever since."

"As I recall, those were your first words to me yesterday," she threw back.

"I never hated you, even though I thought I did. Oh, maybe for a while, but that was because you had shattered my ego by marrying another man so soon after leaving Afton."

His admission made her want to tell him the truth, that far from hating him, she was afraid of what he made her feel and long for. That because of him, her relationships with other men were doomed from the start. "I admit that I left Afton with a heavy burden of guilt. We *are* related through marriage, Wade. I wasn't particularly proud of what I did. I should have had more sense."

"I didn't know pride or sense had anything to with it. We found ourselves attracted to each other. It happened, and there was nothing sinful about it, only what you concocted in that fertile imagination of yours."

"That's easy to say now," she whispered.

"Because it's the truth," he said reasonably, persuasively. "Now that you've reached the venerable old age of thirty, don't you think it's time to stop using hate as the excuse to stay away from home? You certainly have nothing to fear from me. We've both grown up since that summer and ought to be able to coexist peaceably enough."

"I agree."

"So I no longer have to worry that memories of our lovemaking have anything to do with your reasons for not moving back to Afton permanently?"

"Of course not."

A glimmer of satisfaction darkened his eyes. "Good. Then I expect you not to turn down the folks when they put their proposition to you." At the shocked look on her face, he added, "Let's not pretend anymore. You don't have a job yet. There's no reason for you not to stay."

Before she could refute his statement, he had slowed down behind Clyde's car to pay the entrance fee to Teton Park and flashed the attractive female ranger a smile. When the woman reacted openly to his charisma, Kathryn experienced feelings of jealousy, then chastised herself for responding like a lovesick teenager.

Maybe that was what was wrong with her. Maybe she had a case of arrested development. Surely they couldn't have traveled the eighty-odd miles from Afton without her being aware of anything but Wade. Somehow, when she was with him, everything else receded into nothingness. That was how it had always been when she was around him, and the realization terrified her.

"Hi!" Laurel suddenly made an appearance at Wade's open window. "Can I ride with you two the rest of the way?"

"Sure. There's room."

"Thanks. I need a breather." She made a grimace that told its own tale and ran around to the other side of the truck. She hopped in next to Kathryn who was forced to slide along the seat closer to Wade. Inevitably her left arm and thigh brushed against his; her skin seemed to sizzle with the contact. She held herself rigid and tried surreptitiously to ease away an inch or two, enough to prevent touching him.

But every time he had to brake or turn, Kathryn was jostled against him. She prayed he couldn't hear her heartbeat hammering out of control. Fortunately Laurel was so busy exclaiming over the magnificent view of the Teton Mountains Kathryn doubted her niece was aware of the tension filling the cab. She sincerely hoped Laurel didn't notice the way her gaze was repeatedly drawn to Wade's lean bronzed hand palming the gearshift near her knee. More often than not, his fingers grazed her sensitive skin, and she discovered she craved those feather-soft caresses.

When they arrived at the Coulter Bay parking area, she felt a keen sense of disappointment as Wade got out of the cab to help Clyde, depriving her of even that brief intimacy.

The next half hour became a blur of activity. The boat was lowered into the water, and once again Kathryn found herself alone with Wade when the rest of the family made the first run across Jackson Lake to Elk Island. John stood at the helm with an agreeable smile on his face.

"Maybe Dad's talk did some good, after all." Wade's comment coincided with her own private thoughts. For the thousandth time, she was struck by their uncanny ability to read each other's minds.

Kathryn watched until the old motorboat was only a speck in the distance. Inhaling the fresh mountain air, she gazed up at Mount Moran looming over the dancing blue water. There was no sight like it on earth. She opened her mouth to express her feelings to Wade, only to find him studying her upturned face with an intensity that set her pulses racing.

"You love this place as much as I do," he murmured in a low voice. "You'll never convince me you could be as happy living anywhere else."

Because what he said was so true, Kathryn didn't attempt to deny it. Instead she excused herself to visit the general store, needing to put distance between them. When he looked at her like that, she could almost believe he was able to see into her soul. And since she was afraid to analyze those hidden feelings and motives too deeply, she didn't dare leave herself vulnerable to his conjecture.

She went into the little market, bought some groceries she wanted to contribute to the family supplies, then visited the rest room, the last bastion of civilization. There were no facilities of any kind on Elk Island, which meant campers had to bring in absolutely everything they needed. But that was part of the fun and made the trip an adventure.

By the time she went back outside, John had returned in the boat. As she approached, he and Wade were in the process of loading the kayaks and extra drinking water.

"I don't see the parasail," John muttered.

"It's still in the back of the truck."

"I'll get it," Kathryn offered, eager to be of some use. She found it stuffed neatly in a duffel bag and alongside it, Wade's fishing-tackle box and fly rod. In two trips she brought everything to the dock and they were ready to go.

Once they'd cast off, John drove the boat at a wakeless speed toward the buoys.

"Time for your 'Mae West.'" At Wade's words, she looked up to see a grin break out on his face as he lowered an orange life preserver around her neck and shoulders. The unexpected warmth in his lopsided smile made her heart turn over. "In that ponytail, you look about sixteen."

"The sun must have blinded you," she said, unable to prevent a slow smile of her own, briefly forgetting what a dangerous game she was playing. She shouldn't allow herself to get close to him. Nothing had changed. He was still five years younger, with his whole life ahead of him. But even more, he was her sister's stepson, and he was engaged to be married to a woman named Amy. Faced with such indisputable facts, she shouldn't be having this much trouble remembering why she had to stay away from him.

But when she would have turned aside, Wade's eyes narrowed on her softly parted mouth, as if he contemplated kissing her. She stood there helplessly while he proceeded to tie the ends of the life preserver beneath her quivering chin and across her chest.

When John opened the throttle beyond the bay, Kathryn wasn't ready for the sudden lurch of the boat. She fell backward as it plowed through the wakes of the other crafts. Thanks to Wade's quick reflexes, she was caught around the waist in time to avoid a nasty bump on the head.

Later she told herself everything would have been all right if Wade had let her go as soon as she regained her balance. But somehow his hands slid over her hips, drawing her close to him in a quick compulsive movement.

For the space of a heartbeat she melted against him and felt the low groan deep in his throat before he abruptly set her free. In a daze, she watched him work his way between the kayaks to the front of the boat and engage John in conversation, as if she didn't exist.

But for Kathryn, nothing would ever be the same again. Because, despite honor, despite decency and common sense, the sexual attraction for Wade was still there, and infinitely stronger than before.

CHAPTER FOUR

"YOU'RE NEXT, Aunt Kathryn! Everyone else already had their turn!"

While John and Wade were out in the boat, Laurel spread the parasail over the sand, then helped Kathryn into the harness and began fastening the straps.

Three college-age boys in a ski boat had pulled up to shore and were watching them with unabashed interest. One of them called out, "How about the two of you coming for a ride with us when you're through?"

"No, thanks," they shouted back.

"Then what about dinner later on?"

"We're busy," Laurel called over her shoulder.

"We'll show you a better time than those dudes out on the lake."

"If they're not careful, John'll start swinging," Laurel confided with a laugh.

"I wish they'd go away. I haven't done any parasailing for over five years and don't need an audience when I plop in the water instead of taking off."

"It's like riding a bicycle. You never forget."

"That's easy for you to say. You're not as old as I am."

"You don't really feel old, do you?"

"Sometimes," Kathryn muttered. "Especially right now."

"Well, you don't look it, and judging by the way those guys in that boat were flirting with you, I'd say you don't have anything to worry about until you're at least Mom's age."

"Hey, my sister's figure is still fantastic."

"I know. I'm only teasing, but you have to admit she wears her hair funny and won't buy trendy clothes."

"I think Clyde likes her just the way she is."

"He does. It's sickening."

Kathryn chuckled. "You won't think that when you fall in love with the right man."

Laurel's hands stilled on one of the straps. "Are you still in love with Uncle Phil?"

"No. The truth is, our marriage was never a love match like your parents'"

"Why?"

"Because I realized too late that I'd married him for the wrong reasons."

After a moment's reflection, Laurel said, "I hope you won't get mad if I tell you that I never thought you were happy with Uncle Phil."

"So you noticed."

"Only because you acted so different around him than you do when you're with the family. Particularly if Wade happens to be there. That's something I remember from before."

"Wade? What do you mean?" She willed herself not to react in front of Laurel, but at the mention of his name Kathryn heard a buzzing in her ears.

"I don't know. It's not something I can explain, but you've always acted, I don't know, more *alive* around him. You were never like that with Uncle Phil."

Maintaining an impassive expression, Kathryn said, "That's probably because Philip's a good deal older and sort of formal. Wade is still young and he's . . . exciting."

"If we weren't related, I'm sure I'd be in love with him."

"A little hero worship is normal," Kathryn whispered on an unsteady breath. "It's not uncommon with younger sisters."

"Every girl I've ever brought home from school goes crazy over Wade."

"I bet a few have gone a little crazy over John, as well."

"That's true, but Wade is so sexy. Don't you think?"

Kathryn couldn't take much more. "If you want my opinion, everyone in your family is attractive, especially you. I have no doubt there'll be a letter from Steve when you get home."

The change of subject seemed to do the trick, and for the next few minutes Kathryn was treated to a list of Steve Newton's virtues, and Wade appeared to be forgotten.

But not by Kathryn. She couldn't get Laurel's observations out of her mind, nor could she take her eyes off Wade, who was now signaling to her from the back of the boat. While John drove, someone else—a strong swimmer—had to "spot" in case of trouble. Since Clyde and Alice were in their tent and Laurel was needed on the beach to help lift the parasail, Wade was the logical choice.

Secretly she had to admit that if anything did go wrong, she would be thankful he was there to help. Wade was the kind of man other people always counted on, particularly in a crisis.

Furious with herself for allowing thoughts of him to overtake her, she told Laurel she was ready, picked up the rope and gave the thumbs-up signal to Wade. Within seconds John was idling the boat toward open water.

Nervous tension sent the adrenaline surging through her veins as Kathryn watched the lines slowly uncoil. She waited for Wade's hand to fall, and then she started running as fast as she could toward the water, ignoring the shouts and whistles from the boys in the ski boat.

Laurel was keeping pace behind her, and suddenly Kathryn was airborne. The sensation was like experiencing liftoff in an airplane, except that she shivered from the cooler air currents as she flew higher and higher. Once she reached maximum lift, all she had to do was hang there and enjoy the ride.

Gliding through space at this altitude, she had a more intimate view of the majestic Tetons. Below, she could see all of Elk Island with its individual campsites and the surrounding blue water. But inevitably her gaze focused on Wade who watched her through binoculars, waiting for her directives.

She couldn't forget for a moment that his eyes were trained on her. Even high above the jewellike lake she felt connected to him, and she wondered if she would go through the rest of her life in this precarious condition.

As soon as the sun slipped behind the Grand Teton, Kathryn noticed a distinct change in temperature. Deciding she'd had enough, she signaled with her thumbs and immediately John cut the motor. She floated down, enjoying the swaying sensation before she hit the water.

Wade swam toward her and reached her as she surfaced, detaching the chute from the harness so it wouldn't drag her under.

Wolf whistles and clapping greeted her ears the moment her head popped out of the water. The guys in the ski boat drove as close as they could manage. "We'll be by later to take you for a ride," one of them hollered.

"Sorry. I'm not interested."

"Get lost!" John shouted, clearly ready to take matters into his own hands.

Treading water, Kathryn smoothed her long brown hair away from her face, wishing they'd leave. She was astonished at how persistent they were.

"We'll show you a good time."

"The lady said no thanks." Wade's tone sounded forbidding. By this time he was back in the boat, hands on his hips, daring them to say another word. If it had been anyone but Wade, she would have found the situation amusing. But the possessiveness in his voice, in his whole manner, said he was deadly serious. Apparently their visitors thought so, too, because they roared off without further comment.

Kathryn swam to the boat, completely exhausted now. Wade leaned over the side and helped her in. She slid to the floor in an inelegant heap, which for some reason struck her as funny. No doubt the combination of Wade's nearness and the strange turn of events that had suddenly placed her in his orbit had something to do with her precarious state of mind. Whatever it was, her body needed release from the pent-up strain. She started to laugh.

Wade squatted beside her, his mouth quirking in shared amusement. The way he stared at her made her feel as if they were the only two people in the world. "You had a good ride, obviously."

"It was wonderful," she said when her laughter subsided somewhat.

"In case you were worried, your takeoff was better than usual," John teased from the driver's seat.

She had forgotten all about her nephew and turned to him guiltily. "You drove the boat like a pro. Thanks, John."

"I wish I could return the compliment where your driving's concerned," he quipped.

"Don't you know it's not nice to remind me of my flaws?" Still giggling, she made a face at him.

Wade got to his feet, drawing her attention to his hard muscled body and the way his swim trunks rode low on his hips. "Let's get you out of that harness."

"I'll manage." Averting her eyes, she stayed where she was and unfastened the straps, afraid he'd try to help. Afraid to risk any more physical contact with him.

John started the motor and soon they arrived back on shore. Before Wade could offer his assistance, Kathryn climbed onto the railing and jumped to the sand. She waved to Alice, who was busy cooking dinner near the campfire.

"I'll be right there to help you. Just let me change into some dry clothes."

"Wade put up your tent. It's through those trees. And Clyde's rigging a toilet for us farther up on the island, where we had one before."

"Great!"

The perky dome tent stood beneath a shelter of pines and would stay cool throughout the hot afternoons. Though Kathryn wouldn't have minded rooming with Laurel, she much preferred having her own place to sleep. Wade knew her well, too well, but right now she was thankful for his thoughtfulness.

He had also put her bags inside the opening. In a few minutes she'd changed into jeans and a white sweatshirt. Securing her hair with an elastic band, she felt ready to face the evening and realized with surprise that she was hungry.

When Kathryn joined the others, she noticed Wade had been put to work shucking corn, while John set up the portable picnic table. Laurel stood over the charcoal broiler tending the T-bone steaks while Alice stirred a pan of potatoes and onions on the Coleman stove. The marvelous aroma made Kathryn's mouth water. "What can I do to help, Alice?" she asked, studiously avoiding Wade's appraisal as she drew near the fire.

"Would you mind looking for Clyde? We're about ready to eat. I can't believe he's not back yet."

"I'm on my way." There was still enough light for her to see without a lantern. She retraced the steps to her tent and struck out through the underbrush.

A few minutes later she saw the makeshift toilet and eventually came upon Clyde, who stood at the edge of a pond and put a finger to his lips at her approach. Curious to find out what held him captive, she moved as quietly as she could to stand next to him. He draped a friendly arm around her shoulders and together they watched a family of beavers diligently repairing their dam.

"I'm bringing my camera up here in the morning," he whispered. Kathryn nodded and continued to watch, equally fascinated.

"Dinner's ready. Alice asked me to come and get you."

"I'm glad she did, because I've been wanting to have a chat with you when no one else was around. Shall we start walking back?" Was he going to tell her about the apartment they were renovating for her? She hoped not, because her response would only disappoint him, and she didn't want that to happen.

"Am I in trouble?" she teased.

Clyde chuckled. "You sounded like Laurel just now." He patted her arm. "I want to apologize for John's behavior."

She felt almost weak with relief. "That's not necessary. You know I love your children without reservation. Besides, every family has its ups and downs."

"Well, we're in a definite down cycle right now. But that's not what's on my mind. Can we talk honestly for a minute?"

Kathryn slowed to a stop. "Of course. What is it?"

She heard him expel a sigh. "I'll come straight to the point. Did Wade do something to alienate you five years ago? Is that why you never came home for a visit?"

Her head started to pound uncomfortably. "No, Clyde. Wade's always been wonderful to me."

After a long pause he muttered," Alice said you told her the same thing, which means I've figured it all wrong."

"What are you talking about?"

"You left Afton while we were on vacation in Canada, and none of us even got to say goodbye. To make matters worse, Wade wouldn't talk to anybody and took off for Colorado without any explanation. Naturally I assumed he'd said or done something to make you leave so abruptly."

Praying for inspiration, she said, "Nothing could be further from the truth. Since I've always had a hard time saying goodbye to all of you, I decided to go before you returned to save myself additional pain. Particularly since I knew I might be gone a long time to complete my doctorate. I can't speak for Wade, of course, but please believe me when I tell you he's never hurt me. Quite the contrary." Because it was the truth, her voice rang with conviction.

"I'm glad to hear that," he said with telltale gruffness. "I hadn't wanted to believe it of Wade."

"Oh, Clyde, I'm so sorry you've been worried for nothing."

"Are you sorry enough to tell me why you stayed away so long?"

Kathryn was prepared to tell him the truth, at least as much as he needed to know for reassurance. "My marriage to Philip was a mistake from the very beginning. I'm not proud of what I did, because it hurt him so much."

"Honey! I don't believe what I'm hearing!"

"I could never bring myself to confide in anyone about it, especially not you and Alice." Her voice trembled. "He seemed like the kind of man I should marry, so I did. But in time I realized I was never in love with him, and if you want to know the truth, I became . . . indifferent to the physical side of our relationship."

Without any warning, Clyde gave her a long hug. The loving gesture brought tears to her eyes. "I had no idea."

"I know, because I tried to hide it from everyone. But I realized that if I ever brought him home to stay with you, you'd all see what a sham my marriage was. I couldn't bear that, for myself or Philip. You know, Clyde, despite your problems, you and Alice have what I consider the perfect marriage. And coming home to watch the two of you would have been like pressing on the nerves of a sore tooth. It was easier inviting you to the beach where I could pretend to be busy and madly happy."

"Then you deserve an Academy Award, because I never caught on."

She sniffed and wiped her eyes. "Clyde . . . I hold every marriage I see up to yours for comparison. You've made my sister so completely happy, I'm envious."

"And with those kind words, you've relieved me of a great burden." He kissed the top of her head.

"Thank you for confiding in me. Now if I could just get Wade to do the same."

"I—I thought you two were close."

"We were, before he went away to college. Then everything changed. And even though he's been back for two years, he still keeps to himself. When he does make one of his rare appearances, he's aloof, hard to read. And now John's starting to act the same way."

Kathryn was finding it difficult to remain objective. "You know how Wade is, Clyde. When he's interested in something, it's all-consuming. I would imagine the affairs and responsibilities of his ranch keep him occupied. And John's probably suffering from burnout. He's been at the university for three years now, and believe me, you reach a point where you don't know if you're coming or going. I remember it only too well."

Clyde's eyes held a faraway look. "That's true enough, but I have a hunch something else is eating at both of them. I hate to even think it, but I've begun to suspect that Wade's regretting his engagement." His words sent a shudder through her body. "Did Alice tell you we suspect John has a crush on Amy?"

"Yes."

"What a mess!" He rubbed one hand anxiously across the back of his neck.

Kathryn could only echo his sentiments. When she'd first heard about Wade's engagement, it had turned her world upside down. She hadn't been able to comprehend it, and now to hear Clyde express his doubts about Wade's commitment...

"Finally!" Alice called out when Kathryn and Clyde emerged from the underbrush. "What kept you, honey?"

"Beaver dam." With that obscure comment, Clyde bent over and kissed his wife's astonished mouth. "Let's eat," he said when he raised his head. "I'm starving."

"We all are," Laurel murmured. "If the steaks are too well-done, it won't be my fault."

"I'm not worried." Clyde smiled, tousling his daughter's short curls in an affectionate gesture before sitting down on one of the camp chairs placed around the table.

Kathryn found a seat between John and Clyde and concentrated on her steak. Only once did she make the mistake of lifting her head—to discover Wade's speculative gaze on her. Guiltily she looked back down at her plate and started eating her corn on the cob.

Later, as the family lingered over a dessert of fresh fruit, Kathryn jumped up to clear the dishes. Everybody urged her to sit down again, but she refused, explaining that they'd all been waiting on her and it was time she did something to earn her keep.

While they sang campfire songs, darkness settled over the park, and the stars came out, brilliant against the clear night sky. Soon Clyde was terrifying everyone with his spine-tingling Big Foot stories. Though Kathryn stood a short distance away putting leftover food back into the coolers, she was totally absorbed in one of his famous yarns. Suddenly a tremendous crack rent the air, followed by a series of ear-piercing explosions, and Kathryn screamed. Her reaction set off peals of laughter from the others.

"John Matheson, wherever you are, you're going to pay for this!" she shouted crossly. How could she possibly have forgotten John's obsession with fireworks—especially this close to the Fourth of July?

"You'll have to catch me first!" she heard him call.

"I plan to!" With a wicked smile, she reached into the drinks cooler and pulled out a fistful of ice. Fairly certain of his intentions, she ran toward the beach. Sure enough, he was climbing into one of the kayaks to make his escape, cackling all the way.

"Oh, no, you don't!" While he was attempting to shove off, she plunged fully clothed into the warm water and stuffed the ice down his shirt. At his sudden yelp, the laughter on shore grew more raucous.

Not satisfied, she started rocking the end of the kayak to prevent him from getting away.

"I think this is where I come in," Wade murmured over her shoulder, his breath a light caress against the damp skin of her neck. In one effortless movement, he overturned the kayak, pitching John headlong into the water. Laurel was right there with a gleeful smile to tow the kayak out of reach.

Wade unexpectedly grasped Kathryn's hand. "Come on, let's swim for it," he whispered. Before she knew how it had happened, Wade was dragging her through the water toward the opposite shore of the little half-moon bay.

She could hear John's cries of vengeance in the background, but they lost all significance as she swam beside Wade. The moment she could feel sand beneath her feet again, he picked her up in his arms and ran swiftly from shore into the protection of the trees.

He obviously had their old destination in mind. She couldn't think, couldn't even force out a protest, not when her heart was pounding like this. It might all have been a game to him, but Kathryn was no longer smiling. The heat of his body against hers created a longing for him so heady, so intense, she began to feel almost panicky.

When she thought she might do something insane, such as reach up to kiss the mouth she'd been aching for, he stopped running and lowered her slowly to the ground. The friction between their bodies left her gasping with desire, and she broke free of his arms.

"Did I hurt you?" he asked.

She waited for her breathing to return to a semblance of normal. "No. I'm just winded because I'm out of shape."

Through the trees she could see two kayaks headed in their direction, with John in the lead. "They're coming," she said, shivering in the coolness of the night air.

"But they won't find us. They've never discovered our hiding place yet." She felt his hands gather her hair to wring the water from it. His touch made the blood pound in her ears, and she actually thought she might faint.

"Do you think it's wise to provoke John?" she asked weakly, hoping to distract him—and herself. "You know how much he hates being bested by anyone."

Wade's fingers twisted in the glistening brown strands, which gave off the faint flowery scent of her shampoo. "That's a strange question coming from someone who thought nothing of tipping him over in the kayak a few minutes ago. Why this sudden concern for him?" he drawled. "I noticed you and Dad took your time about getting back to camp tonight. Care to tell me what that was all about?" His question might have sounded casual, but she heard the steel in his tone.

"We were watching the beavers."

"But that doesn't exactly preclude conversation, does it?" His question was rhetorical; he obviously knew very well something had gone on between her and Clyde. Wade had always been too observant for her peace of mind. He'd certainly know she was lying if she pretended not to understand him.

"As a matter of fact, John did come up in the discussion." As she spoke, she tried to back away so he'd release her hair, but he didn't.

"There was one, then."

Taking a shallow breath, she said, "He's worried about his family, like every father."

"What did he say to make you so quiet at dinner?"

Kathryn didn't dare reveal that their conversation had centered mainly on Wade. "Nothing specific. But our talk made me realize that being a parent is a tremendous responsibility."

In the distance she could hear Laurel yelling at John to wait for her. Already their kayaks had touched shore.

"Did he tell you John's in love with my fiancée?" When Kathryn looked away, he muttered, "I thought so."

"Actually I figured it out for myself at dinner last night."

"John has always been transparent."

Dry mouthed, she whispered, "What are you going to do?"

"What do you think I should do?" he countered softly.

"When you picked me up at the airport," she lashed out, suddenly panicking "you made it clear you didn't want to discuss your personal life with me."

"Things have changed since last evening. Don't you agree?"

"W-why don't we sneak toward shore and surprise them?" she asked instead, incapable of answering his question. The question that lay at the heart of her grief.

"Why don't you answer me?" he demanded forcefully. When she refused to say anything else, his fingers seemed to tighten in her hair. "Why does the thought of John's involvement with Amy create such alarm in you? It's not so surprising. They're both young, the same age, and they have a good deal in common."

She swallowed hard. "Did I say I was alarmed?"

"You don't have to say anything. Your body's doing it for you." A strange smile illuminated his face. "I'd like to hear how you think I should solve my dilemma. It's no secret that you and I have always had an affinity for each other and that we've often shared similar views." He paused. "You know, I used to rely on your opinions, especially about what other people were thinking, how they felt. I want your ideas about this situation with John."

"I haven't been around for five years, so you're asking the wrong person."

"Why do you feel ashamed to admit there's a bond between us that has nothing to do with time or distance?" His voice had taken on a seductive quality, which confused her.

"I'm not ashamed." Her voice wobbled, as much from the insistent caress of his hands in her hair as anything else.

She heard the tempo of his breathing change. "I honestly believe you're frightened. Why?"

"Don't be absurd. But I am worried that if we stay hidden any longer, John and Laurel will get upset. I refuse to be responsible for creating friction if I can help it."

Tossing her head so he'd have to let go of her hair, she darted through the trees toward the two figures searching the beach for signs of her and Wade. Waiting till their backs were turned, she raced for the closest kayak and shoved it into the water. Once she was inside she yelled, "Thanks for the transportation, guys!" Then she started paddling madly back to the camp.

She heard John's bark of disbelief followed by Laurel's laughter, and suddenly John was on her trail in the other kayak. Midway across he drew alongside her and slapped the paddle in the water, practically swamping her. "That'll teach you to play around with the big boys."

"I think you've forgotten what a big girl I am," she baited him, relieved that he still wanted to play. Using her paddle, she gave the water a resounding slap of her own, but the splash wasn't nearly as spectacular. He mocked her efforts, and his grin was the last thing she saw before he overturned her kayak.

Getting into a kayak without tipping it was one thing. Crawling out of it, upside down, underwater was another, and for some reason she was finding it particularly difficult to extricate herself. After several seconds she began to worry because her tennis shoe seemed to be caught. No matter which way she twisted, she couldn't pull herself loose.

Just as she began to feel light-headed, a sure pair of hands freed her foot and she was propelled to the surface with astonishing speed.

She drank in gulps of air before slumping against her rescuer, momentarily spent by the ordeal and weak with fright. "Thanks John," she sighed when she could catch her breath. "I was starting to panic."

"You're safe now," he answered hoarsely. Only it was Wade's voice that resonated through her system, Wade's strong body absorbing the convulsive tremors of hers beneath the water. Her eyes flew open.

"Are you all right, Aunt Kathryn?" John and Laurel cried in unison, swimming up to her and Wade. Verging on hysteria, Kathryn put her hands against Wade's chest and pushed herself away, forcing a smile to her lips as she treaded water.

"I'm fine," she assured them, avoiding Wade's unsettling gaze.

"I'm sorry, Aunt Kathryn," John murmured solemnly. "I thought you were swimming underwater to get away from me."

"That was my intention." She winked.

Laurel still looked upset. "What happened?"

"Her shoe wouldn't clear the lip of the opening," Wade explained grimly.

John's expression sobered even more. "I had no idea you were still underneath."

"If it had been you who overturned, I would have thought the same thing," she said in an attempt to alleviate his guilt. "Remind me to remove my shoes the next time I get the urge to steal your kayak."

John stared hard at Wade. "Thank God you saw what was happening!"

Kathryn couldn't tolerate any more emotion. "Come on, Laurel. Let's beat these guys in a water fight before we turn in." She felt safe in suggesting it, since they were only about thirty feet from shore, so the water was fairly shallow at this point. "But this time no tricks and no weapons. Hands and feet only!" To emphasize her words, she chopped the water with the edge of one hand, sending out a spray that soaked all of them afresh.

"You're on!" Laurel laughed and joined in, imitating Kathryn's actions with effective results.

"You little devil!" John proceeded to dunk his sister, but their playful antics made no impact on Kathryn, who could feel the tension emanating from Wade like a tangible thing.

His face was hard, emotionless. "I don't know about you, but I've had all the water sport I can handle for one night." With that quelling remark, he struck out for shore, cleaving the water with lightning speed.

Needing to channel the energy building inside her before it exploded, Kathryn joined Laurel in her playful fracas with John. Five minutes later he'd had enough, and they worked their way to shore with the kayaks, completely exhausted.

Alice and Clyde were sitting by the fire when they got back. At first Kathryn was afraid Wade might have said something about her near-drowning. But judging from their relaxed quiet mood, she could see that wasn't the case. She breathed a little more easily.

While Alice passed out mugs of hot chocolate, Clyde doused the embers of the fire for the night.

Kathryn saw no sign of Wade and assumed he'd gone to his tent, something else to be grateful for.

After washing her mug, she hugged Alice, then muttered good-nights to everyone else. She hurried to her tent by the light of a huge white moon shining overhead. It was going to be a long night....

CHAPTER FIVE

THOUGHTS OF WADE and the closeness they'd once shared prevented Kathryn from falling asleep for hours, despite her exhaustion. Consequently she didn't waken until eleven the next morning. She discovered she'd been lying on top of her sleeping bag because the tent was so warm.

Except for birdsong, everything was quiet. When she stepped outside, she saw that the boat was missing and realized she must be the only one still in camp. Taking advantage of the solitude, she heated some water on the Coleman stove for a sponge bath, then dressed in a clean pair of shorts and T-shirt. To keep the hair out of her face, she fashioned it into two ponytails, one over each ear; she didn't bother putting on makeup but sprayed herself liberally with mosquito repellent. Since she was hungry, she decided to cook a fabulous lunch and surprise everyone when they returned to camp.

Occasionally a boat drove into the little bay while she was slicing the onions and peppers for steak fajitas. She hoped she wouldn't have to put up with another visit from those guys in the ski boat. But then she remembered how effectively Wade had dealt with them and decided she didn't have to worry.

Smiling to herself at the fierceness he'd shown, she walked over to the cooler to get the tortillas. When she lifted her head, Wade was in her line of vision. He was strolling up the beach, and she found herself staring not only at the symmetry of his movements, but at his well-muscled body clad only in a pair of white cut-offs, which accentuated his deep tan.

She was so mesmerized it took her a second to realize he was alone. Flustered, she hurried back to the Coleman stove and slapped several tortillas on the grill pretending to be too occupied to notice his approach.

"Whatever it is smells fantastic. When do we eat?" Wade was standing only a few feet away.

"Right now if you'd like." She finally dared to brave a glance but regretted the impulse when she saw the way he was appraising her face and figure. The intensity of his regard ignited a fire inside her. "How long have you been up?" she managed to ask.

"About an hour."

His disinclination to talk made her nervous. "Where are the others?"

"Laurel went waterskiing with friends. Dad and Allie are out in the boat observing nature, and far as I know, John's still in his tent."

"In that case I'll call him and we'll eat."

Wade shook his head. "Let him sleep. He's still a growing boy."

If he was sending her a signal that he, Wade, had long since passed beyond that stage, then as far as Kathryn was concerned, he was wasting his breath. She had stopped thinking of Wade as a schoolboy years ago. That had been the problem all along. He might have been five years younger, but mentally and emotionally, she had always felt he was her equal. And when they had started making love, he became the tutor and she the pupil.

"Kathryn? You didn't hear what I said, did you?"

Heat stained her cheeks. "What?" She was furious that her thoughts had once more centered on him to the exclusion of all else.

"I was asking if you'd like to go for a ride in the boat when the folks get back. If we're lucky we might see some moose over by the point."

It was a perfectly reasonable suggestion, and if the situation had been different, she would have welcomed an opportunity to explore the lake. But the bittersweet pain of being with Wade had rekindled that once familiar ache, the sharp sensation of a desire that craved assuagement. She felt far more vulnerable now than she had five years ago.

"I think the whole family would enjoy that. Maybe by the time we're finished eating, Laurel will be back and she and John will want to come with us."

"Maybe." But his tone conveyed that he knew she was afraid to be alone with him and, worse, that he found her reaction amusing.

"How many fajitas would you like?" She reached for a paper plate, amazed she could still function more or less normally.

After a strained pause he said, "Two ought to do it."

"Sit down at the table and I'll serve you."

He drew a couple of colas from the drinks cooler before following her suggestion.

"They're hot, so be careful you don't burn yourself." Once she'd carried his meal to the table, she fixed another plate for herself and sat down opposite him.

Though there was an uncomfortable silence between them, he seemed to be eating with considerable enjoyment, and she derived a ridiculous amount of pleasure from that. "These are delicious," he verified minutes later, raising his head. "I want the recipe."

"I'll give it to your wife for a wedding present." She had to keep reminding herself that Wade belonged to someone else.

"Much as she'd appreciate it," he countered smoothly, "I was thinking of the cook I'm going to hire when my dude ranch is operational. Good meals are one of the critical features. The success of the whole enterprise will depend on repeat business, and food like this will help persuade people to come back for more."

Wade never said what he didn't mean, which caused her to cherish his compliment. It was frightening how badly she wanted his approval. "I'm glad you find the food to your taste."

He stared at her, an odd expression on his face. "You learned to make these in California, didn't you?"

For some reason she began to feel uneasy. "That's right. We entertained various members of the faculty and visiting professors on a regular basis, so I was continually challenged to come up with something different."

"Do you cook anything else as good as these?"

She laughed a trifle nervously, because he was being so serious. "You really want to know?"

"I wouldn't have asked otherwise." As he spoke, he seemed to find her mouth of inordinate interest. His scrutiny made it hard to concentrate.

"I suppose it depends on your preference."

"What did Philip like?"

"Philip?" She repeated the name in a daze.

His jaw tensed. "Your ex-husband," he reminded her unnecessarily. "What was his preference?"

She took a deep breath. "I don't recall exactly."

"Most wives would know the answer to a question like that."

"Maybe," she murmured, and looked away, feeling the usual rush of guilt for having hurt Philip. "But he has gourmet tastes and likes a variety of exotic dishes."

She was relieved when Wade dropped the subject and went over to the stove to get another fajita. But when he came back to the table he said, "Did you meet the man you got involved with at one of your dinner parties?"

"What did you say?" she demanded indignantly. The fork she was holding slipped from her fingers and clattered against the table.

"You heard me," he replied without sounding at all disturbed by her anger. "Is that how it happened?"

"How *what* happened?"

"In the truck on the way to Afton, I asked if you'd had an affair, and you didn't give me a satisfactory answer."

"Because a question like that doesn't deserve one," she replied, white-faced, and rose from the table. But he put a detaining hand on her arm, forcing her to remain where she was.

"You're still the most attractive woman I've ever met, but the breakup of your marriage has done its damage. Maybe divorce wasn't the solution, after all. Would you go back to him if he'd have you?"

"Who?"

"Philip, of course."

"No!" On that point she'd been honest with everyone else in the family and could be no less with him. "Does that answer your question?"

His fingers tightened painfully on her wrist. "Because you're in love with someone else?" His eyes seared hers, demanding a response.

"If I am," she retorted angrily, "it's absolutely none of your business."

"Are you?" he persisted, refusing to be put off.

Kathryn had had all she could take, and the physical contact was making matters worse. "All right!" she practically shouted at him. "If it'll satisfy this unhealthy interest of yours in my love life, I'll tell you. Yes! I'm in love with someone else!"

Too late she realized what she'd done. She'd told him the truth; couldn't deny her feelings any longer. *She was in love with Wade.* The soul-searching kind of love that would haunt her for the rest of her life.

A stillness crept over him and the skin on his cheeks went a dull gray beneath his tan. "The baby wasn't Philip's was it?" His hand had become a vise around her wrist. "Did you fall in love with a married man? Is that why coming to Afton is such a penance, because you can't be with your lover? Is that the reason Philip won't give you any more alimony?"

"Let me go, Wade," she said through clenched teeth, stunned at the depth of his faulty suspicions and at the intensity of his response. He acted as if her answer *mattered* to him. And that was absurd, considering that he was in love with another woman. "I've had all the cross-examination I'm going to take from you."

Adrenaline lent her strength and she jumped up from the table, wresting her hand from his grasp. But she hadn't counted on the momentum propelling her backward.

He cried her name as she crashed into the camp chair and landed flat on her back in the dirt. Somewhere in another part of the camp she heard John call out, but nothing registered except the feel of Wade's hands framing her face.

"Are you all right?" The concern in his voice belied his earlier hostility. Confused by his contradictory behavior and the touch of skin against skin, she pushed his hands away and got to her feet.

"I'm fine," she said on a shallow breath, wiping the dirt from her shorts. She was furious that their little altercation had disturbed John, who was now racing toward them. Things had become so complicated that all she wanted to do was run away. She needed to be alone somewhere, to come to terms with this impossible situation.

"What happened?" John looked from Kathryn to Wade, who had plucked the chair from the dirt and was examining it. "I heard shouting."

"I'm not surprised," she inserted before Wade could say anything. "We were eating lunch when my chair suddenly toppled over and he tried to save me." She flashed John an ingenuous smile. "Sorry to have disturbed your sleep, but now that you're up, do you want some fajitas?"

"If they're the same kind you made us at the beach, lead me to them, woman!"

Kathryn laughed and felt some of the tension ease out of her. "Do you have any idea how much you sound like Clyde? Sit down and I'll serve you."

Now that Wade couldn't continue his probe into her personal life, she assumed he'd find something else to do. But he surprised her by handing John a root beer from the cooler and making himself comfortable in one of the camp chairs placed around the table.

"Thanks," John said, squinting at his brother. "Have you tasted her fajitas already?"

"I had three, and now I'm thinking of hiring her to be my cook at the ranch." She could feel the exact moment Wade's gaze shifted to her. "How about it, Kathryn? You can consider this a bona fide job offer. It'll help me out, and your unemployment problem will be solved."

Uncaring of the fragile ground they walked on, she said, "Sorry, Wade. Flattered though I am by your confidence in my culinary abilities, I'm not interested." Wearing her brightest smile, she continued, "In the first place, you couldn't afford me."

She regretted her words even before she noticed how Wade's features had hardened. He suspected she'd married Philip for his money, and her comments only reinforced that idea.

"And the second?" His voice sounded like the lash of a whip.

"Since I won't be in Afton much longer, this discussion is pointless."

John frowned. "What are you talking about?"

"I'm applying for a permanent teaching position in Colorado. I plan to see about it next week." Though she hadn't made the decision until that very moment, she knew it was the right one.

"But you can't! You'll spoil the surprise!"

"She already knows about the apartment," Wade told him without any inflection in his voice. "Obviously it makes no difference."

John shook his head. "Mom'll be so disappointed. One of the reasons we came on the trip now rather than later was to keep you from the store so the carpet could be laid and the furniture delivered before we got back. She and Dad wanted you to have your own place as soon as possible."

"You're kidding!" She didn't need to feign shock. Wade hadn't hinted that the apartment was ready to move into.

"No. And that's not all. Because you used to help out in the store, Dad hoped he could talk you into working for him this summer, or at least until you have concrete plans for the future."

Kathryn averted her eyes from Wade, who continued to gaze at her with an enigmatic expression while John did all the talking.

"You might as well hear the rest. Mom misses you a lot more than you realize. She and Dad have been hoping and praying you'd return to Afton for good. They've talked of nothing else ever since they heard you were getting a divorce and leaving California. Their plan is for you to live over the store rent-free and they'll pay you a salary. But naturally they're not going to try to talk you into anything you don't want."

These revelations, coming so hard and fast, made everything that much more painful. The love Alice and Clyde had always shown Kathryn was never more evident than now. And if it weren't for Wade, she'd gladly take what they were offering and even look into obtaining a math position at the local high school for the next academic year. But the way she felt about Wade made it impossible for her to consider their plan.

As if talking about Clyde and Alice had conjured them up, there they were, walking along the beach, looking ridiculously relaxed and happy. Clyde was crooning one of his favorite old songs, and his broad smile was so reminiscent of Wade's, Kathryn wanted to cry. "We're back, we're hungry," called Clyde, "and something smells too good to be true."

She couldn't believe she hadn't heard the boat, because the motor made enough noise to wake the dead. Now that John had told her the truth, just looking at their smiling faces made her feel worse than ever. Feigning lightheartedness, she waved her arm over her head and called back, "Then by all means, come and get it!"

Within five minutes Laurel had arrived back at camp, as well. For the next half hour Kathryn avoided Wade's scrutiny while she made more fajitas for the rest of the family.

Eventually Clyde got up from the table and stretched. "That was the best food I've ever tasted."

"You say that after every meal." Kathryn smiled.

"That's because you and Alice outcook anyone in Star Valley." His comment came too close on the heels of the conversation she, Wade and John had just had.

Afraid to look at Wade, she mumbled her thanks, then quickly started clearing the table.

"Since you made lunch, I'll do the dishes," Alice stated matter-of-factly, reaching for the plastic tub, but Clyde forestalled her.

"It's time the men did the cleanup. You wanted to take a nap, so why don't you go to the tent? I'll join you as soon as I'm through here."

To everyone's surprise John said decisively, "Since I slept in till noon, I'll do the dishes."

Clyde staggered backward in an exaggerated gesture. "Do my ears deceive me? Did my son actually say he'd let his old dad off the hook?"

"Yeah." He flashed his father a begrudging smile. "Go have a nap. But don't expect this to become a habit."

"I wouldn't dream of it." Clyde chuckled and tossed the keys on the table. "If anyone wants the boat, it's available."

"I don't." Laurel looped her beach towel around her neck. "My friends are coming by a little later, so I'm going to sunbathe till they get here."

As the three of them went on their way, Wade picked up the keys. "So, Kathryn, that leaves you and me."

Her heart lurched, because she knew what was coming. Out of self-preservation she would fabricate any lie to avoid being alone with him. She didn't think she could hide her feelings for him much longer. "I need to make a few calls from the marina," he said.

"Do you want to come with me? On the way back we'll run by the point."

She shook her head. "Thanks for the invitation, but right now I feel like a little physical exercise. I'm going to take a walk around the island. Maybe we can all go for a boat ride this evening."

A taunting smile lifted the corner of his mouth. "Until later, then." Wade's response might have sounded innocent to John, but she heard his implicit threat—that he wouldn't be satisfied until he'd learned the name of the man who had contributed to the breakup of her marriage.

Even though she was thankful he hadn't pressed her to accompany him, she was shocked by the sense of desolation that swept over her as she watched him stride swiftly toward the shore. Soon the boat was speeding out of the bay toward open water, taking him farther and farther away from her. More than anything in the world she wanted to go with him, be with him, have the right to live with him and love him for the rest of their lives.

"I imagine he's going to call Amy," John murmured, jerking Kathryn from her thoughts. She'd forgotten she wasn't alone, and right now she didn't want or need John's assessment of the situation, even if he, too, was suffering.

Purposely ignoring his comment, she said, "After the dishes are done, what are you going to do with the rest of this gorgeous day?"

"Get my tackle together and do a little fishing in the kayak."

"Be sure and catch a German brown for me. In return, I'll search for huckleberries—I know how much you love them on your pancakes."

Without waiting for a reply she grabbed an empty plastic bag from the camping supplies and struck out on her own. Her body cried for release from the frantic energy that had been building ever since she'd seen Wade walking toward her outside the airport terminal in Salt Lake City.

Determined to stay away from camp until she could be certain of not finding herself alone with Wade, Kathryn spent the rest of the day gathering the purplish-black berries. Her hunt took her all over the island, which teemed with squirrels, hedgehogs, woodpeckers and beavers. But she found little peace in the beauty and harmony of nature. What cruel trick of fate had decreed she live an unfulfilled life because of a forbidden love?

Her thoughts kept returning to the incident in the boat the day before, when Wade had caught her around the waist to prevent her from falling. For a breathless moment his hands had dropped to her hips, creating a heat that had nothing to do with with the temperature of the air.

Nor could she forget the intensity in his eyes while he was tying her life preserver. Her mouth could almost taste his, because for that brief instant, she knew he had wanted to kiss her. And God forgive her, more than anything else in the world she wanted to feel his lips caressing her own.

The sun was setting when she returned, sunburned and tired, to the campsite. Dazedly she lifted her eyes to John and Laurel, who were out in the kayaks, but nothing really registered, because thoughts of Wade were all that filled her mind and heart. She searched avidly for him and saw his crouched figure farther down the shore. He was cleaning fish, his dark blond head bent in concentration. To Kathryn, everything about his body was perfect. Desire for him welled up in her till she could have cried out for his touch.

As if he sensed her need, he unexpectedly raised his eyes. They stared at each other, unsmiling, until she found the strength of will to turn her back on him. Nothing in his unswerving regard revealed what he was thinking, but she was very much afraid he had read too much in hers. She could have wept at her lack of control.

Clyde exclaimed over the huckleberries, then told her to relax because dinner wouldn't be ready for a while. Since he didn't require help, Kathryn started through the pines toward her tent and bumped into Alice.

"Oh, good. You're back! I was just about ready to send out a search party for you. My heavens, but you're sunburned. Why didn't you put on some screen?"

"Would you believe I forgot?"

Alice sighed. "Oh, Kathryn. Well, come over to our tent. I've got some medicated spray that should help."

After Alice's ministrations, Kathryn sat down opposite her sister in one of the camp chairs placed outside the tent. She could see the Grand Teton clearly through the pines, it's snow-capped summit tinted pink and crimson by the sunset. The sight never failed to thrill her.

"Finally I've got my little sister to myself for a few minutes. There's been so much going on we haven't had time for one of our good old heart-to-hearts."

"I know. All of us being together has meant the world to me," Kathryn admitted emotionally.

"Clyde is happier than I've seen him in years. Did I tell you he's sold a couple of articles to some fishing and wildlife magazines?"

"No! When did that happen?"

"About a month ago. And they pay well for accompanying photos. He's such a natural in the outdoors, his expertise shines through despite his inexperience in writing. Luckily Wade's been able to help him polish his manuscripts before they were sent off."

"Wade was always good in English."

Alice smiled. "Let's face it. Wade can do anything. Maybe I'm prejudiced, but I know that one day his ranch is going to be famous. He's always had the right instincts about things. Haven't you noticed?"

Kathryn made a sound of assent, too wrapped up in her own thoughts of Wade to express anything concrete.

"He was born confident," Alice went on. "I'm convinced that with the right woman, there isn't any dream Wade can't achieve, and Clyde agrees."

Struggling for breath, Kathryn said, "Do you like Amy? Will she make Wade a good wife?"

Alice stared intently at Kathryn. "Honestly? Do you really want to know?"

CHAPTER SIX

THE FACT THAT Alice answered her question with another made Kathryn uneasy. "When have we ever been anything other than honest with each other?"

"Since you left the house five years ago without saying goodbye. Since the time you ran off to Mexico to be married without sharing one of the most important moments of your life with your family. Since you remained in an unfulfilling marriage for more than four years without confiding your pain to a living soul. And—" Alice paused, her blue eyes staring boldly into Kathryn's "—since you insist you want to go to some strange town as a university professor when I know in my heart you'd be happier teaching math here, married to a wonderful man and raising a family. How's that for starters?"

No one could see through Kathryn like her sister. "I thought we were talking about Amy."

"If you want to discuss her first, we can do that. She seems to have everything a man could want in a woman. Ask John and he'll tell you. Interestingly enough, the more time passes, the more I'm convinced Wade's not in love with her. As for Amy, I think she's young enough to be in love with love and is somewhat confused by John's attention.''

Kathryn's heart leapt with unholy joy, but she had to hide her feelings from Alice. "Spoken like a true mother."

"And what about you? Wade's happiness is obviously important to you, or you wouldn't be so anxious to know what kind of wife Amy's going to make."

"Naturally I want things to work out for him, and I understand your concerns about Amy because I wasn't in love with the man I married and I wouldn't wish that on Wade of all people," she said in a tremulous voice. "Even so, Amy must be quite exceptional to have captured his interest in the first place."

There was a brief pause. "He admires her horsemanship and the fact that she doesn't take herself too seriously." Alice heaved a sigh. "Maybe I'm crazy, but I had this idea that when Wade fell in love, he'd be like Clyde. You know how his eyes light up sometimes when we're looking at each other?"

"I should imagine the whole world knows," Kathryn teased, causing her sister to grin.

"The fact is, I've never seen Wade look that way at Amy. I think if I ever did, I wouldn't have a worry in the world."

Kathryn knew exactly what Alice was talking about, because Wade's eyes had once blazed for her with that special light. She felt her body grow feverishly hot as she recalled that look of his—the look that said he wanted to be alone with her all night long, wanted to make love to her until they forgot everything and everyone else in the wonder of being together.

What was really incredible was that even now, knowing Wade was engaged, the selfish part of her didn't want him to be involved with Amy, let alone make love to her.

"Come to think of it, I can't remember the last time I saw *your* eyes sparkle," Alice went on. "It must have been before you left for San Diego. Which brings me to the reason I wanted to talk to you alone. Please consider what I'm about to say very carefully."

Kathryn closed her eyes, knowing exactly what her sister was leading up to.

"I think you need me as much as I need you. We're family, and the older I get, the more sentimental I seem to become. When you wrote and told me you and Philip were breaking up, I asked Clyde if we could convert the storage area above the store to an apartment for you, so you could come home to a permanent place of your own."

"I—I know," Kathryn cut in before Alice could say more. "Between John and Wade, I was told everything. Promise me you won't be angry with them."

Alice's pretty face broke out in a smile. "If they chose to reveal our little surprise ahead of time, then you must know how much it means to the family to have you back here to stay."

"Alice..." Kathryn found herself getting choked up. "I've always loved you, looked up to you. And I love Clyde. You're two of the kindest, most unselfish people I've ever known. I don't deserve all the sacrifice and expense you've gone to for me. I—hardly know what to say." Tears streamed down her cheeks. She was humbled, moved by their generous loving offer, but her feelings for Wade were in the way.

"Just say yes." Alice leaned forward and covered Kathryn's hand with her own. "After what you've been through, you need a complete change of pace and a more relaxed life-style. We want to help. That's what families are for."

"But—"

"I know what you're going to say," she interrupted. "You have a career to think about. I understand that. And I've already talked to the superintendent of the school district here about getting you a teaching position. When he heard your credentials, he said he could guarantee you a job in the fall, because good math teachers are hard to come by. If it doesn't work out, you could always apply for a university position next summer. What harm would there be in living close to us and teaching high school for a year?"

What harm would there be? Kathryn cried inwardly. Being around Wade was a torture she couldn't endure much longer.

"Look," Alice continued. "Will you do me one favor before you make a final decision?" Kathryn nodded reluctantly. "Next week is our twentieth wedding anniversary. Because we went to Banff on our honeymoon, Clyde wants to take me up there for a week."

The irony of the situation wasn't lost on Kathryn, who had to stifle a groan. The mere mention of the Canadian town triggered a flood of guilty memories, all having to do with that disastrous time five summers earlier when the rest of the family had gone to Banff on vacation, leaving her alone in the house with Wade.

Alice, however, seemed totally unaware of the emotions surfacing in Kathryn and said, "Would you consider staying in the apartment and working at the store with Laurel and John until we get back? They both adore you, and frankly, knowing you'd be around for them to talk to would be a big relief to Clyde and me. And the apartment would give you the privacy you need.

"If, after we get back, you still feel you have to pursue a career in Colorado, then we'll support you. But please remember the apartment is legally yours and will always be here for you."

Kathryn sprang from the chair and threw her arms around Alice. "No one ever had a sister like you. I love you and Clyde so much. Thank you, thank you for everything." After another round of tears and hugs, Kathryn stood up and wiped her eyes.

She couldn't possibly refuse her sister's request. If she did, it would only raise more questions in Alice's mind. But Kathryn knew she'd be risking further grief and heartache. Her only consolation was that working in the store meant she wouldn't have to see Wade very often. And she had to assume Amy would monopolize his free time.

"Of course I'll stay while you're gone. You deserve a second honeymoon free of worries."

"I knew I could count on you." Alice was positively beaming.

"The thing is, though, for my own peace of mind, I need to interview for a teaching position in Colorado right away, if only to find out what's available. Why don't I fly to Denver as soon as we get back home from camping? In a couple of days, I can visit both campuses, talk to the heads of the departments and return to Afton before you leave on your trip to Canada."

Alice studied Kathryn's face for a brief moment, her eyes revealing little of what she was thinking. Finally she said, "I can't argue with that logic, and your plan coincides perfectly with Laurel's. She and her friend Cindy are driving to Salt Lake to see the 'Days of 47' celebration."

"That's right! The twenty-fourth of July is only a few days away."

Alice nodded. "They can drop you off at the airport and pick you up from your return flight. Cindy's aunt lives in the city. She's going to let them sleep over—then they can go to the parade and the rodeo."

"In that case, I'll drive to the marina in the morning so I can phone ahead for plane reservations and set up appointments."

"Good." Alice got to her feet. "Now that we have that settled, I'm going to see if Clyde wants any help preparing dinner."

"While you're doing that, I'm going to freshen up before dinner. I'm a mess."

"That'll be the day." Alice smiled. "Take your time. I'll tell you when it's ready," she called over her shoulder as she headed for the cooking area.

Kathryn went to her tent, feeling a strange lethargy that made every step seem an effort. Evidently the conversation with Alice, following her long hike in the hot sun, had taken its toll. By the time she reached the tent and sat down on her sleeping bag, she scarcely had the energy to take the rubber bands from her hair and brush it. In fact, the urge to lie down became too strong to ignore. Thinking she'd only rest for a few minutes, she stretched out on her stomach, still holding the brush in her hand.

Until she heard someone say her name, she knew nothing else. At first she thought she was dreaming, but a man's voice called to her a second time, and when she recognized it, she came awake instantly.

"Wade?" With pounding heart she sat up, blinking into the darkness. "I must have fallen asleep. What time is it?" she asked through the closed tent flap. She was glad he couldn't see her.

"Midnight."

"I don't believe it! Is something wrong?"

"I was about to ask you the same question. When we called you to dinner, you were out like a light. Allie said you spent too long in the sun, so we decided not to disturb you. But that was hours ago, and since I'm the last one to go to bed, I thought I'd check on you in case you wanted anything,'' he said in a low voice.

"Thank you, but I'm fine. I guess I forgot that the sun's more potent at this altitude than at the beach."

"If you're hungry or need to go use the privy, you can take my flashlight. Clouds have moved in and I saw sheet lightning a few minutes ago. We'll probably have a storm before long."

"Lightning?" When she was a little girl, Kathryn's father had been killed by lightning in a pasture. Though she and Alice had eventually overcome their phobic reaction to it, Kathryn had never felt completely at ease during an electrical storm and preferred not to be alone when one occurred.

Wade must have remembered other storms in the past when he had stayed home to comfort her, and it explained why he'd awakened her now. He hadn't wanted her to wake up, suddenly and alone, to the frightening sounds of a storm. His thoughtfulness shouldn't have surprised her, but she was still disoriented from sleep and feeling far too vulnerable where he was concerned.

"Shall we sit it out in my tent or yours?" he asked wryly. "We both know you won't get any more sleep until the storm passes over."

A clap of thunder helped make her decision. She scrambled to her feet and quickly unzipped the mesh

and the tent flap. Wade shouldered his way in, bringing wind and the smell of rain with him.

While he made everything watertight again, Kathryn climbed into her sleeping bag, still wearing her
shorts and T-shirt. Wade turned on his flashlight and
beamed it in her face, which was partially hidden by
her loose hair. She felt his probing gaze before he
propped the flashlight in the corner to light the tent.

"Here." Avoiding his eyes, she handed him her extra blanket. "You'll need this to sit on."

He spread it at the foot of her sleeping bag. The tent
was built for three, so it easily held them both. In a
lithe move he lowered himself to the blanket and
tossed her an apple.

She bit into it, guiltily relishing the situation—the
cozy confines of the tent and Wade sprawled at her
feet. "Mmm. This tastes good. Thank you. I didn't
realize I was hungry."

He said nothing, and for an uncomfortable moment, simply stared at her.

In the space of a heartbeat, the brief camaraderie
she had felt with him was gone. In its place was a pal-
pable tension that charged the atmosphere and made
it impossible for her to act naturally. She put the half-
eaten apple on the ground beside her. Though she
could see lightning flashes outside the tent window,
her nervousness stemmed from a different source entirely.

Another clap of thunder cannonaded across the
lake, much closer this time, and a cold wind whistled

through the pines, signaling that rain was imminent. As if Wade could read her mind, he reached above him and zipped the window closed.

Unconsciously she watched the play of shoulder muscles, the effortless grace that was as much a part of him as his clean male scent, and sun-darkened skin. She could still remember the feel of his powerful body against hers after he'd rescued her from the overturned kayak the night before. She forced herself to look away.

He resettled himself on his side and faced her, propping his head on one of her duffel bags. "Is it true what Allie told everyone tonight?"

She knew what he was talking about and couldn't pretend otherwise. "If you mean that I'm going to stay in Afton and work at the store while they're away, then yes."

"Why?"

His response shouldn't have hurt, but it did. "Because I promised Alice I would," she said hotly. "I'm surprised you'd even ask that question, since you were the one so adamant that I go along with their plans."

"It's obvious that being separated from your lover is making you miserable," he said. "How's he going to react when he finds out you're stuck here longer than you'd anticipated? It wouldn't surprise me if you'd been planning to meet him in Colorado—were you? Is that why you're so eager to get there? If so, why prolong the agony?"

His questions, fired one after the other, coincided with the first drops of rain spattering the tent. In the glow of the flashlight, she studied the lines and angles of the rugged features she loved so well. She averted her eyes and took a deep breath. "I have no intention of meeting him in Colorado or any other place—he belongs to someone else."

Wade sat up and his eyes gleamed like a cat's. "But you're still in love with him."

"Yes," she admitted in a husky whisper. Oddly enough, telling Wade the truth was her best defense. As long as he assumed she was talking about another man, it made the situation easier to handle.

"If that's the way you feel, why don't you go back to California and do something about it?"

"Because there are insurmountable problems."

"Nothing's insurmountable if you want it badly enough." His voice was surprisingly harsh.

"It is when he's devoted to another woman."

Wade's mouth twisted in derision. "How devoted could he be if he got involved with you to the point that your husband asked for a divorce?"

"You don't understand, Wade." She shook her head helplessly. "There are other considerations of equal gravity."

"Name one."

"I'm not prepared to go into them."

"Was the baby his?"

For the life of her she couldn't understand his interest in the baby. "No, because I never slept with him.

Philip was the father of my unborn child, and that's as much as I'm willing to tell you."

A long pause ensued, and she noticed that the rain had become a steady downpour.

"Then what are you saying?" he asked tersely. When she didn't answer right away, he muttered an oath. "Does this man even realize you're in love with him?"

"No."

His brow furrowed. "Why in the hell not? Don't you think he'd want to know something that important?"

"Would *you?*" she retorted without thinking. "You're engaged to be married!" Her chest heaved with the violence of her emotions. "How would you feel if a female acquaintance suddenly bared her soul to you? What if she revealed her obsession with you, not giving a thought to anyone else's feelings? Wouldn't this woman be complicating your life in all kinds of ways, just to gratify her own needs and desires? How would Amy like it?"

"I'm the wrong person to ask," he murmured. "If a love that overpowering came into my life and I reciprocated the woman's feelings, then I'd never let her go. Naturally I'd break my engagement to Amy, because it wouldn't be fair to her."

Kathryn wasn't certain if the tremor rocking her body came from the ground or within herself. But one thing was perfectly clear. *Wade wasn't in love with his fiancée.*

What had driven him to propose to Amy when his deepest emotions weren't involved? Alice and Clyde had voiced the same concern, but Kathryn, more than anyone, could recognize the situation for what it was. She'd traveled down that empty road herself—and she'd taken Philip with her.

Suddenly she thought she knew the answer and felt the blood drain from her face. Was it possible that his relationships with other women lacked the fire she and Wade had once found in each other's arms? Maybe he was making the same mistake she'd made with Philip. Maybe he was willing to settle for less. Maybe he'd become engaged to Amy because she seemed to be the kind of woman he *should* marry—and because she wasn't Kathryn.

"It's a good thing your fiancée didn't hear you say that, or she might not understand."

An eternity seemed to pass before he said, "Would you care to elaborate on that statement?"

His anger frightened Kathryn and she lowered her head. "I—I shouldn't have said anything. Please forget it."

"That would be impossible."

"The storm is over. You don't need to baby-sit me any longer."

"Is that what I'm doing?"

Growing more uneasy in his presence, she edged farther away from him and felt the wall of the tent at her back. "Wade, I'm sorry. I had no right to say that."

Somehow he had moved closer. "But you did, and I have no intention of leaving until you explain exactly what you meant."

She swallowed hard. "I was merely implying that I expected you to say something like, 'Amy's the great love of my life so the possibility of responding to another woman, no matter how much she professes to love me, simply doesn't exist.'"

There was an unnatural quiet before he said, "Does the man you love qualify as the great love in Kathryn Lawson's life?"

"Yes," she answered without hesitation.

"Even if he never knows the truth?"

"There's such a thing as honor."

"Honor be damned. It's more than possible he's in love with you. You have an obligation to tell him how you feel, for both your sakes."

"No."

"Then you're a fool and you deserve every second of misery life brings you."

"Thank you," she whispered and jumped to her feet, unwilling to let him see the effect his words had on her.

"Kathryn, for the love of heaven, come back here!"

But her only desire was to escape. The problem was she'd forgotten just how quickly Wade could move. Before she reached the tent opening, he grabbed her by the shoulders and twisted her around to face him, his rugged features in shadow.

"So help me, Kathryn, don't you know the only reason I said that was because I know what a passionate woman you are?"

His mouth was too close, too tempting. The touch of his hands sent a paralyzing warmth through her body. She turned her head away, trying to hold on to her sanity. "That was a long time ago, Wade."

"Are you saying passion is wasted on the young? That you're no longer capable of it? Why don't we test out that theory to see if it's true?"

"No!" He grasped her forearms and she fought him in earnest. But pushing her hands against his chest was a mistake. With his superior strength he easily trapped them against the weight of his body, then drew her into his arms until there was no space between them.

She tried turning her head to evade him, but his hands checked her movements. With the accuracy of a heat-seeking missile his mouth locked on hers, releasing a charged energy that had been stored deep inside her for five long years and was bursting to be spent.

She knew it would be like this if he ever touched her again, that every particle, every cell, every atom of her body would explode into unquenchable flame.

Terrified because she wanted to be lost in that chaos of feeling but knew it was wrong, she gasped, "No more," and tore her lips from his.

But Wade easily held her in place, demonstrating his physical mastery over her. She had to look away from the arrogant curve of his mouth, the mouth that had brought her alive in a fresh, painful way. How could she have allowed this to happen?

"So, now we know you're not in your dotage quite yet," he taunted softly. "After blowing that theory to bits, I can't help but wonder what else we might uncover with a little more experimentation."

"Get out, Wade!" He had driven her to the breaking point and he knew it.

"I'll leave when I'm ready," he warned in a voice taut with anger. He reached for the flashlight and beamed it on her face. At her cry of surprise he lifted his other hand and with his thumb sensuously brushed the swollen softness of her lips, which still bore traces of the passion they had shared.

"Just so we understand each other, don't start psychoanalyzing me and my feelings unless you're prepared to undergo more of the same scrutiny yourself."

"I'll never let you touch me again," she whispered fiercely. But her declaration came too late, because he had already left the tent.

Smothering a sob, she flung herself on top of her sleeping bag, wishing she could howl out her anguish. Five years away from Wade should have killed her feelings for him. But that hadn't happened. And the desire he aroused with one smoldering kiss changed all the rules.

What was she going to do? What *could* she do until she left Afton for good?

Knowing how relentlessly Wade pursued anything he wanted, she would have to go to extraordinary lengths to avoid being alone with him.

There would be no more sleep for her that night. Thanks to Wade, the blood coursed hot and heavy through her veins, reminding her that she was a woman deeply in love, wanting to express it in the age-old way. But he was forbidden to her, forever out of reach. When she contemplated the emptiness of a future without Wade, scalding tears trickled out of the corners of her eyes.

She spent the remaining hours of the night devising a scheme to keep herself out of his way. By the time morning came, she was armed with a battle plan and knew exactly what had to be done.

CHAPTER SEVEN

KATHRYN WAS UP with the sun and took it upon herself to prepare a breakfast of bacon and pancakes for any early risers. It was no small feat, since she had to remove all the damp tarps protecting their stores from the rain the night before.

Except for a few puffy clouds, the sun shone brightly this morning; everything would be dry by noon. As she'd hoped, John emerged from his tent first. He was exactly the person she needed to carry out her plan.

After making a sound that must have meant good-morning, he sat down at the picnic table. "How did you know I was dreaming about pancakes dripping in huckleberries?"

"Because they've been your favorite since you were old enough to smear them all over your high chair," she teased.

He helped himself to half a dozen. "Do me a favor and never tell that story in the presence of company."

Kathryn chuckled. "I promise." She brought the bacon and orange juice to the table and sat down next to him. "What's on the agenda today?" She needed to elicit information from him without arousing suspicion. "I'm embarrassed to admit I was so tired last night, I fell asleep before dinner."

"After we ate, everyone went to bed, but I heard Dad say he and Mom are going to laze around the camp all day and do absolutely nothing."

Kathryn started eating her pancakes. "If that's the case, why don't we wake up Laurel and the three of us can go waterskiing while the lake's still calm? Afterward I'll treat you to late lunch over at the lodge on Coulter Bay."

"Sounds good to me. What about Wade?" he asked with his mouth full of juicy huckleberries.

Striving for a steady voice, she said, "Oh, he's not all that keen on skiing. He'd rather fish from his kayak. If we leave, it'll give your folks a chance to be alone together."

John nodded. "Shall I get her up?"

"No. I'll do it. You finish eating."

Laurel loved the idea. Within half an hour, the three of them had taken off in the boat, leaving a note, carefully secured by a rock, on the picnic table. If Wade was awake and heard their activity in the camp, he didn't come out of his tent to investigate. Neither did Alice or Clyde.

For the first time in three days, Kathryn was able to relax and play and fully enjoy the company of niece and nephew. It reminded her of times at the beach, when there had been no Wade to disturb her thoughts.

After they'd ordered their lunch in the dining room of the lodge, Kathryn slipped out to the reception desk and made several phone calls. With that accomplished, she joined her niece and nephew for roast-beef sandwiches.

At around three that afternoon, Kathryn suggested they fill the gas tank and return to camp in case Alice and Clyde wanted to use the boat. On their way back, Laurel drove past the point to see if Wade had caught any trout for their dinner. But his kayak wasn't there, which produced contradictory feelings of relief and deflation in Kathryn.

As the boat glided in to shore, she spied her sister and brother-in-law sunbathing on a blanket. Both kayaks were present, which meant Wade had to be somewhere in the camp. The pulse at the base of her throat began to throb with a nervous excitement she couldn't suppress.

The five of them chatted for a while. Kathryn learned that Wade had taken the camera to see if he could get some more nature shots for Clyde. She decided this was a good time to go fishing—primarily so she wouldn't be in camp when Wade returned. When she mentioned the idea to Clyde, he suggested they all climb back into the boat and troll off the point for their dinner.

John declined, wanting to do nothing more than cast from shore. But Laurel was game, and Kathryn couldn't have been happier with the plan. The four of them set off with their fishing tackle and didn't come back until dark. They'd caught enough trout for two dinners; what they didn't eat, they would take home with them in the morning.

After they returned, Kathryn purposely stayed close to Alice while they fixed dinner. Asking her sister a string of rapid-fire questions about former acquaintances living in Afton gave her an excuse to ignore Wade. He was cleaning their catch and chatting quietly with his father about the possibility of a magazine article on moose.

Everything seemed pleasant enough on the surface. But the very fact that Wade hadn't once talked to Kathryn or even flashed her a glance kept her on edge. She was definitely glad she'd stayed away all day.

With dinner over and the dishes done, she lighted a Coleman lantern and asked to be excused, claiming she had a good book to read. When she bent to kiss Alice good-night, Clyde reached for her free hand. "A ranger was here earlier today and he told us to prepare for more thunder showers. Until I saw Wade at the door of your tent last night, I forgot you tend to get as nervous as Alice. If things are bad, feel free to come to our tent," he said loudly enough for everyone to hear.

"Thank you," she whispered and gave him a peck on the cheek, hoping he couldn't feel the heat radiating from her face. Nothing escaped Clyde. Her greatest worry now was wondering how much of their conversation he might have overheard the night before.

Maybe this was his way of letting her know he didn't approve of Wade's going to her tent alone in the middle of the night. If that was the case, he was not only covering for Wade's actions in front of the others, but warning him off. Or worse, maybe he was chastising *her* for allowing Wade entrance. Likely he did suspect something irregular, considering his worry over what had happened five years before.

That thought deepened her guilt, and she refused to look at Wade, whose gaze she seemed to feel boring into her back. Murmuring a quick good-night to everyone, she hurried to her tent and prepared for bed, but couldn't concentrate on the new paperback she'd brought.

Questions went around and around in her head, making it impossible for her to sleep. A little after two in the morning, the predicted storm began. It was every bit as intense as the one the night before, but for the first time in years, she was plagued by dark disturbing thoughts that frightened her a great deal more than the elements. She stayed in her tent.

By morning she'd come full circle in her thinking. She'd decided that Clyde would never have urged her to stay and work at the store if he suspected anything too seriously wrong. Still, his remarks of the previous evening troubled her, and she determined to be circumspect in every step she took around Wade from now on.

Fortunately the breakup of camp kept everyone busy, and after breakfast Kathryn dismantled her own tent so there'd be no reason for Wade to offer his help. From the corner of her eye she could see him working at a steady pace. But the set of his features revealed his taciturn mood, and she noticed everyone giving him a wide berth.

When they'd loaded the boat for the first trip to the marina, she arranged to ride with Laurel and Alice. While John went back to the island to pick up his father and Wade, Kathryn slid into the rear seat of Clyde's car. She had no intention of driving home with Wade, not for any reason. And judging from his sullenness, he would find her company equally objectionable.

Eventually the men got the boat onto the trailer and stowed the rest of the gear in the back of Wade's truck. As John took his seat next to Kathryn, Clyde and Alice gave Wade a hug, which he reciprocated before climbing into the cab. He took off without so much as a backward glance.

Watching his truck disappear from the parking lot, Kathryn felt a stab of unaccountable remorse, as if he'd taken part of her with him.

"Whew. Wade's been in a nasty mood since yesterday," Laurel murmured when her parents got into the car. "What do you suppose is wrong with him?"

Clyde grunted something unintelligible, but he looked worried as he started the engine and pulled away from the marina. After a minute he said, "Right now he has a great deal of responsibility at home."

"Your father's right," Alice added. "Wade's under a lot of pressure to get his ranch operational."

Kathryn stared out the window, pretending she didn't know the real reason for Wade's anger.

"It's hard to go back and face reality after such a fabulous trip," Clyde was saying. "I know, because I've had about the best time of my life with all of you. I wish it could go on indefinitely."

At that point Laurel and John agreed it had been one of the family's better vacations, because their aunt Kathryn had been with them.

For the duration of the journey home, they talked about Kathryn's new apartment, which would probably be ready for occupation upon her return from Colorado. By the time they arrived at the house, Wade had already deposited their gear in the kitchen and left for the ranch. Kathryn knew she should have been grateful for a respite from the strain his presence created. Instead, she felt a sense of mourning, a sense of irreplaceable loss. She couldn't shake the moroseness that shrouded her throughout the next two days, not even when she was working in the store and waiting on tourists who needed everything from sunglasses to fishing lures.

The family showed her the apartment above the store, which was conveniently located off the main highway. Although small, it was well designed with a cozy living room, bedroom, bath and kitchen. Kathryn loved the dollhouselike feel and thanked them repeatedly for their wonderful gift. If it wasn't for Wade, she knew she could be happy there.

As it was, she had to pretend indifference to him and his situation, while inside she missed him so badly she thought she'd go crazy. Neither Clyde nor Alice seemed inclined to discuss him in front of the family, so Kathryn suffered in silence. Worst of all, she was continually tormented by images of him and Amy sharing intimacies she could only dream about.

Her despair deepened and she found herself looking forward to the Colorado trip. If she didn't get away soon, she feared she might weaken—might drive over to the ranch to see Wade. She simply couldn't let that happen. Being with Wade for those three days and nights in the Tetons had made her realize how *vital* he was to her. Now she was suffering from a sort of withdrawal, she supposed, and the pain was growing more acute.

Early Tuesday morning, Laurel and her close friend, Cindy, drove Kathryn to Salt Lake City's airport, where she boarded a plane for Denver. There, she rented a car and traveled to Boulder for her first interview, which went even better than she'd expected. The head of the math department turned out to be one of her undergraduate professors; he seemed delighted to see her again and praised her credentials.

Though he couldn't make any promises, he believed a teaching position might become available for the second semester, starting after Christmas. But if it didn't materialize, he could probably offer her a post beginning in September of the following year. In any event, he would write her by mid-August and let her know.

She thanked him for his time, and after visiting a few old haunts, drove to Fort Collins where she stayed the night at a motel close to campus. The next morning she had an interview with the acting head of Colorado State University's math department.

This session seemed to go well, too. The man told her he'd definitely like to have her on staff. If she could wait until the second semester, there would likely be an opening. He promised to stay in touch.

Kathryn went back to Denver reasonably satisfied that in time she'd be able to rescue her career. But the knowledge didn't give her any pleasure.

Her impossible love for Wade had blighted her world, leaching away any hope of real joy. She returned to Salt Lake in a stupor of thought. During the drive home, Laurel and Cindy asked questions and Kathryn responded but the conversation barely touched her.

When they finally reached Afton and pulled up at the house, Kathryn caught sight of a gleaming red BMW parked in the drive. Laurel darted her a meaningful glance. "That's Amy's car."

Kathryn felt her heart plummet to her feet. *Wade was inside the house with his fiancée!* In a panic she said, "Why don't we run Cindy home first?"

Laurel blinked. "She's staying over, remember?"

"That's right," Kathryn murmured. "Sorry. I'm afraid my mind has been on those interviews."

Laurel focused concerned blue eyes on her aunt. "Are you all right, Aunt Kathryn? You don't look very good." Cindy agreed.

"I'm just tired because of all the running around I've had to do since yesterday morning."

"You ought to go right to bed," Laurel urged sympathetically, sounding very much like Alice.

Kathryn kissed Laurel gently on the forehead. "Maybe I will. Thanks for everything," she whispered. "I really appreciate it."

"No problem." Laurel grinned. "The next time you want a lift to Salt Lake, just say the word. Cindy and I love an excuse to take off." But anything Kathryn might have said in response faded as Clyde came out the back door. A welcoming smile wreathed his face, though she noticed that it didn't reach his eyes. "Now that you're home safe and sound, I can relax." He put an arm around Laurel's shoulders and tugged on Cindy's braid. "How was the parade?"

"Fine, but it was hotter than last year," Laurel replied. "I guess Mom's still at her sewing club?"

He nodded. "She should be home pretty soon."

"Are Amy and Wade inside?"

After a slight hesitation he said, "No, not right now."

"Well, then, after we unload we're going to walk over to Cindy's for a minute, but we'll be right back."

While the girls carried their things into the house, Clyde helped Kathryn pull her bag and briefcase from the car. "I want to hear all about your interviews, but there's something I have to do first."

Kathryn knew this had to concern Wade, and a strong sense of foreboding prompted her to ask what was wrong. "You looked worried when you came outside," she added.

He let out a deep sigh. "Well, it seems Amy hasn't heard from Wade since she went to Florida and then she couldn't get him on the phone after she returned. So she decided to drive over to the ranch and surprise him. When he was nowhere to be found, she stopped by the store. John immediately asked me for time off to help her find Wade." He looked at his watch. "That was two hours ago and they still aren't back."

Kathryn's guilt about her last encounter with Wade made her feel weak, and she had to lean against the car to steady herself. In a quiet voice she asked, "Do you know where he is?"

He shook his head. "I haven't seen or talked to him since we said goodbye at the marina. He could be anywhere in the valley. Normally he spends the evenings on his accounts, which leaves his days free to work at the ranch." Clyde's eyes shifted to hers and he gazed at her the way his son often did when he wanted answers. "Sometimes I think you know him better than I do. If you have any idea where he might be, I'd like to hear it."

Every time Clyde commented on her relationship with Wade, she grew more panicky. "The one thing I remember about him from the past is that if he had a problem, he either went climbing in the mountains or took off on his horse."

Clapping his palm to his forehead, Clyde groaned, "His horse! Why didn't I think of that? I'm going to drive to the ranch and see if Satan's still in the barn. One way or another, it'll tell me something. I won't be long."

He gave her a peck on the cheek and got into the car. As soon as he'd disappeared down the highway, Kathryn hurried into the house, wishing for the hundredth time that she'd never come back to Afton. From the moment she'd arrived on the scene, everything seemed to be going from bad to worse.

Dead tired and aware of a terrible thirst, she opened the refrigerator, pulled out a cola and stood at the counter to drink it. Once she'd drained the can, she felt fortified enough to go upstairs and prepare for bed, even though she knew she'd spend another sleepless night thinking about Wade and the hopeless situation in which she'd become embroiled.

She sighed in disgust when she looked down at the crumpled white cotton dress, which had been fresh when she put it on that morning. Her hair was spilling from its usual tidy knot and her skin was damp with sweat. Craving a shower, she picked up the things she'd plopped on the floor and headed for the stairs.

No matter what was happening in this household, she didn't plan to be a part of it. She had every intention of hiding in her room until morning. But as she reached the foyer, Wade unexpectedly walked in through the front door and she froze in midstep. He must have come from a business dinner of some kind, because he wore a beautifully tailored summer suit that closely matched his dark blond hair. She swallowed hard, thinking she'd never seen him look so formal or sophisticated. A compulsion stronger than common sense drove her to meet his gaze.

The quiet was deadly. "Well, well," he muttered, "you actually came back. How soon are you leaving us for greener pastures?"

Jolted by his harshness, she snapped, "Apparently not soon enough for you. Now if you'll excuse me—"

"And if I won't?" he taunted. She realized he was challenging her to continue upstairs—because he knew her body would brush against his as she passed him.

"Amy is in Afton, in case it escaped your notice."

"It didn't." He shrugged. "A car like that would be hard to miss."

His brazen unconcern provoked her beyond caution. "Right now she and John are out scouring the countryside for you! Not to mention that your father's driven all the way over to the ranch looking for you. It would've been thoughtful if you'd left word of your whereabouts with somebody."

"You forgot to mention Allie."

Her head flew back. "I can't believe you said that."

"Since you're about to flee this humble nest, your opinion doesn't count for much. The fact is, I don't normally give the family a blow-by-blow account of my hourly business activities. And I can't help it if Amy chose to drive up here and surprise me. I specifically told her before she went on her trip that I wouldn't be able to see her until next week."

Though his explanation sounded reasonable enough, she was far too riled to let it alone. "Then I feel sorry for her. If I were your bride-to-be, I'd have difficulty with a fiancé who managed to stay so unavailable."

His wintry smile mocked her. "Well, if you were, we sure as hell wouldn't still be hanging around here. But you're not, are you? You're my beloved aunt Kathryn, admittedly over the hill now you've turned thirty, and a little the worse for wear because the man you want apparently doesn't want you."

"I think maybe you've had too much to drink," she said through clenched teeth.

Before she could protest, he'd taken hold of her arm and was dragging her up two flights of stairs, bags and all, until they reached his old room. Pulling her inside, he backed her up against the closed door and cupped her flushed face in his hands. The bag and purse fell to the floor with a thud.

"Now tell me again I've had too much to drink," he demanded with his mouth unbearably close to hers, his breath so sweet, so familiar, her senses swam.

"Let me go, Wade," she begged, turning her head away from him. But her movement only served to reveal a smooth expanse of golden skin where the lapels of her dress opened at the neck. "No! Don't touch me," she half sobbed, but it was already too late, because his lips were grazing the scented hollow of her throat. Every moist kiss he pressed against the soft vulnerable skin demanded another, and another. Suddenly her glossy brown hair came loose, cascading over his hands.

"Dear Lord," she heard him whisper on a ragged breath as he took the fatal step that brought his hard body tight against hers. "You feel and smell divine. I want you, Kathryn."

Then his mouth was on hers. In a desperate attempt to free herself before he discovered the truth of her feelings, she went limp as a rag doll, remaining passive to his advances, praying he would finally let her go.

But she hadn't counted on the tenderness, the sensuality of his kisses. With a whimpering moan, she found herself starting to respond to the excitement he created with each insistent caress of hands and lips. Somehow she lost sight of the reasons they shouldn't be touching and holding each other. She was so tired of fighting her feelings that she began kissing him back, sliding her hands inside his suit jacket and around his warm solid body to get closer still.

Her capitulation brought a shuddering response from Wade, who picked her up in his arms and carried her the short distance to the bed. Everything was happening exactly as it had five years ago. Once again, she was lying on his bed, entwined in his arms, and she felt as if her heart were streaming into his. Their mouths fused in an almost violent passion brought on by the long years of separation and triggered by that explosive moment of lovemaking in her tent.

When the knock on the door came, neither of them was prepared for it. Kathryn dragged her mouth from his while Wade groaned over the interruption and buried his face in her hair.

There was something so possessive about the way he held her, she had the wanton urge to let herself go, to let herself love him without restraint or inhibitions.

"Aunt Kathryn? Are you in there?"

A hot blush crept over her face and neck.

"Y-yes, Laurel."

"I'm sorry to disturb you, but Mom's back and she's dying to talk to you. I told her you might be too tired from your trip to join us."

"No. I'll be right down."

"Okay. I'll tell her. By the way, did you see Wade before you came upstairs? His truck is out front."

At the mention of his name, he raised himself on one elbow and stared at Kathryn through eyes still glazed with desire, his fingers entwined in her hair. She felt a wave of shame. *If the family could see them now!*

"No."

Hating herself for lying, she tried to roll away from him. But he covered her mouth with his own, immersing her once again in mindless sensation. Finally he allowed her to pull away from him, and she stood up from the bed as fast as she could.

"That's odd," Laurel muttered, still outside her door. "I wonder where he is. Kathryn?"

"Maybe he left something in the boat and is out in the garage looking for it," Kathryn suggested. She felt distinctly light-headed; Wade had gotten up from the bed and came to stand behind her, wrapping his arms around her. Their bodies were so close she could feel every breath he took, every strong heartbeat.

"Maybe. I'll look. See you in a minute."

As Laurel's footsteps retreated, Kathryn shivered in reaction and his arms tightened. "Let me go," she whispered in a shaky voice. Another minute and she wouldn't have the strength to deny him anything.

"On one condition." He spoke in that familiar authoritative tone.

"Alice is waiting!" she cried. Somehow she managed to wrest herself from his embrace and turn around so she was facing him. It was safer that way.

"Let her," he fired back, unmoved. "We have to talk. Alone. I'll come by for you tomorrow evening after work."

"Aside from the fact that we have nothing to say to each other, the family won't understand."

"We were saying so much to each other on my bed just now, it's a miracle we even heard Laurel. As for the family, when I tell them I want to show you the ranch, they'll think it's only natural."

She shook her head. "What about Amy?"

"She won't be there."

"Don't pretend you don't know what I'm talking about."

"I'm afraid you're the one who takes top honors in that department. I'm going back to the ranch now and Allie will tell Amy where to find me."

Kathryn bit her lip in anguish. "Please, Wade," she implored frantically. "Don't make everything more difficult than it already is." She took a deep shuddering breath. "How can you treat Amy this way?"

His features hardened. "Surely that's my business. Now, what's your answer?"

Her hands tightened into fists at her sides. "I wouldn't put it past you to make a scene, so, yes, I'll be ready when you come by for me tomorrow. But I think you're despicable!"

"That's not the message you were sending before Laurel interrupted us," he reminded her, moving aside to let her open the door. As she darted from the room, his warning trailed after her. "Don't even think of breaking your promise to drive out to the ranch with me tomorrow...."

She was still weak and disoriented from their passionate interlude when she came down the stairs. She'd taken a few minutes in the bathroom to run a brush through her hair and apply fresh lipstick.

Wade had managed to get downstairs ahead of her, because he was standing at the front door talking to Alice, their heads bent together in concentration. Though Kathryn tried to slip unobtrusively from the foyer, she didn't miss the searing glance he sent her. Ignoring it, she headed for the kitchen, where the girls were snacking on pizza.

Just when she thought things couldn't get much more out of control, a distraught-looking John came in through the back door. He stopped short when he saw everyone. "Hi! When did all of you arrive?"

"A little while ago," Laurel mumbled between bites.

"How long has Wade been here?"

"I don't know. You'll have to ask Mom."

He said something unintelligible under his breath and went right back out again. Kathryn hurried after him.

"John?" she called as he was getting into his car.

He wheeled around. "What is it?"

"If you feel like talking, I'm available."

His handsome face screwed up in pain. "This isn't something I can discuss, but thanks, anyway."

He was polite enough, but his words cut like a knife. Perhaps, like his father, John had seen Wade come to her tent that night in the Tetons and had drawn his own conclusions. If that was true, then she couldn't blame him for thinking she and Wade had betrayed Amy, as well as everyone else.

While Kathryn mulled over that very real possibility, John drove off, leaving her standing there as bereft and torn as she'd ever been in her life. It was all growing so ugly she didn't have the faintest idea how anything could be resolved—without destroying the entire family in the process.

CHAPTER EIGHT

"THANK HEAVENS it's closing time!" Laurel exclaimed as she shut and locked the shop door after the last customer. Kathryn's nerves were stretched to the breaking point. All day she'd been fearing this moment—fearing it and waiting for it. Fortunately Laurel hadn't seemed to notice, because they'd been busy since early morning; a steady stream of vacationers had made personal conversation impossible.

Kathryn rang out the cash register to account for the day's receipts. "From the looks of it, business has never been better. Clyde ought to be thrilled."

Laurel paused in her task of replenishing one of the shelves with heavy-duty flashlights. "I know. But he's too worried about Wade to care about anything else right now."

Her comment jolted Kathryn, and she made an error in addition, which necessitated starting the whole process over again. Before long she would be alone with Wade, and the mere thought produced so many conflicting emotions she couldn't respond to her niece.

"Don't you think Wade's been acting weird lately?" Laurel pressed. "I can't begin to figure him out!"

"Like your folks said in the car, he has a lot on his mind."

Laurel shook her head. "I just don't get it."

"What?" Kathryn asked casually, hoping to hide her inner turmoil.

"It's obvious he isn't in love with Amy."

"You don't know that, Laurel."

"I know Wade. He treats her like he treats me."

"I thought he treated you like royalty."

"He does, but you know what I mean. John acts a hundred times more amorous around her than Wade does. I'm afraid Wade's going to marry her and then end up divorced like you and Uncle Philip. It makes me sick just thinking about it."

"It's his life, honey." She had to say something, anything, to distract her niece, who was far too insightful for Kathryn's peace of mind.

"He's bored already. I can tell."

"Who's bored?" a familiar voice countered from the back of the store. Kathryn's heart plunged to her feet for the second time in two days. Neither of them had heard Wade come in.

Laurel's face turned scarlet. She flashed Kathryn a signal of distress. "Don't you know it's not nice to eavesdrop on people?" she snapped.

"Then you shouldn't gossip so you can't be found out," he quipped, and tousled her dark curls lovingly. He must have come directly from the ranch, because he was wearing an old T-shirt and jeans he'd obviously been working in all day. He was still un-shaven.

Yet for some reason Kathryn found him every bit as appealing as she had last night, when he was perfectly groomed. She longed to rub her cheek against the faint shadow covering his jaw and chin, and felt her palms moisten at the thought.

"What are you doing here?" Laurel sounded un-characteristically sharp.

"I came to get some supplies I need and I thought maybe Kathryn would like to drive back to the ranch with me. She hasn't been out there yet." He pinned Kathryn with a level gaze Laurel couldn't see, daring her to defy him. "How about it? Would you like a personal tour?"

Kathryn was grateful that Laurel would never know the real reasons for his seemingly innocent and spon-taneous invitation. "I thought you'd never ask," she teased to cover her chaotic emotions, wanting to shake that self-satisfied expression from his face.

"Am I invited, too?"

Wade gave Laurel an engaging smile. "I thought you were going to the county fair with Cindy to-night."

"I am," she muttered. "I forgot."

Kathryn could feel her niece's curious glance and studiously avoided it by turning off the register.

"Think you can close up here by yourself, kiddo?" Wade asked.

"I've done it for years now," Laurel said ungraciously.

Kathryn felt an awkward silence and walked over to put an arm around Laurel's shoulders. "Thanks, honey. I'll help you out whenever you want to get away early. Tell Alice to expect me home in about an hour. I'll help her pack for their trip in the morning."

"Make that three hours," Wade interjected smoothly. "We're stopping for groceries so I can fix dinner. Let's get going."

This time Laurel's gaze was definitely speculative as she watched Kathryn follow Wade to the back of the store. Once they were outside, Kathryn hurried ahead and got into the cab before he could assist her. She didn't take another breath until Wade drove the truck onto the highway.

"Relax," he admonished, as if this was an everyday occurrence.

"You shouldn't have come while Laurel was still there," she said angrily.

"Since when is it a sin to walk into the family store for a chat?"

Kathryn didn't bother to answer. On the surface, there was no explanation that made sense, and if he refused to acknowledge the reason for her guilt, what more could she say? She preferred to remain quiet during the short drive to the ranch, staying in the truck while he went inside the local grocery store for supplies. For once, Wade seemed to be of a similar mind and didn't torment her with a discussion of what had happened the night before. But she knew it was only a matter of time.

After leaving the highway north of town, they traveled almost a mile along a dirt road lined on both sides by flowering meadows. Eventually they came to a gate with a large wooden sign welcoming visitors to the Circle M Ranch. It signalled the beginning of Wade's property.

He reached for a remote control above the sun visor and pressed a button. The gate swung open; as soon as they'd driven through, it clanged shut again. She heard its echo inside her head, underlining the fact that for the first time in her life she was alone with Wade on his own territory. And as long as that gate remained locked, no one could disturb them. A thrill of fear coursed through her veins because she knew she'd passed the point of no return.

Before long she spied a cluster of log cabins, which appeared in immaculate condition, and a little farther on, a prosperous-looking barn with the Circle M insignia painted in red, black and white beneath the eaves. When they drove past it she gasped softly at the sight of a rustic home made entirely of logs and built in a stand of jack pines. The Salt River was visible in the distance. Puffy clouds sailed overhead, frosted a pale pink by the late-afternoon sun, which was just beginning to dip below the horizon. Kathryn couldn't imagine a more idyllic setting.

"Your house is beautiful! And it's so much larger than I'd imagined."

"I plan to have a big family one day." His voice was even and matter-of-fact, but his statement conjured up visions in Kathryn's mind she knew she shouldn't entertain. But the desire to have Wade's baby had been her secret obsession for five years.

He pulled to a stop alongside stacks of timber, insulation and myriad other building materials. "The main floor is pretty well finished, except for the painting. The upstairs rooms and the basement still need drywall, and that'll take until next summer to complete."

Kathryn jumped down from the cab, eager to explore on her own. "Is the front door locked?" she called over her shoulder.

He shook his head. "No. Make yourself at home while I unload the truck."

She felt his eyes on her back as she picked her way through the obstacle course to the porch stairs. Once inside, the first thing she noticed was a huge stone fireplace that dominated the large living room. She presumed the area to the left of the foyer was intended as the dining room, but there was no furniture as yet.

She walked through a set of double doors into a spacious modern kitchen furnished with every conceivable device, from a microwave to a pasta-maker. Wade certainly hadn't stinted on anything. She smiled at the ancient-looking card table and chairs placed at the far end of the room.

From the kitchen she wandered down a hall and came to a bedroom with an adjoining bath, which he had commandeered. She would have known it blindfolded, by the clean familiar scent of his soap.

Realizing where her thoughts had wandered, she retraced her steps to the living room and discovered a study behind it with built-in bookshelves, another fireplace and a picture window that revealed the flowering meadows in their summer glory. There were file cabinets, a desk, a computer and printer, everything he needed to manage his accounts.

An oil painting of the Tetons hung above the stone fireplace. Curiosity made her walk over to the mantel where half a dozen photographs of the family stood displayed. But her eyes were riveted on one picture in particular. It was of her, alone, taken on a family outing in the Tetons that summer five years ago.

With unsteady hands, she picked it up and studied herself. She barely recognized the smiling curvaceous woman who was posing for Wade as he snapped pictures along the trail.

Quickly she put it back in place, afraid to reminisce about a time that could never come again. It suddenly occurred to her that there were no pictures of Amy. Most likely Wade kept some in his bedroom, Kathryn told herself. She hadn't noticed any when she'd peeked in there earlier, but then she hadn't searched his room thoroughly for fear of being caught.

The sound of footsteps heralded Wade's entrance, and she wheeled around to see him standing in the doorway watching her with a sober expression. "Well, what do you think?"

She drew in a deep breath. "Your home is sensational."

"I'm rather partial to it myself, but I've got a long way to go."

"But that's part of the excitement, isn't it? To see it all come together, bit by bit?" Taking a calculated risk, she asked, "Does Amy love it?"

His brows met in a forbidding frown, and she knew immediately she shouldn't have mentioned his fiancée. "I didn't bring you here to talk about Amy. If you want something to do while I shower, I've brought in the groceries."

After he left, she stood there with her arms folded, trying to calm the quickened beat of her heart, wondering how she was going to make it through the rest of the evening.

Deciding she'd go crazy if left alone with her thoughts, she found her way back to the kitchen and emptied the grocery sacks. Among the purchases were a couple of steaks and the ingredients for a green salad. She took severed potatoes from the refrigerator, scrubbed them and put them in the oven to bake. Then she got busy preparing the salad.

Some time later, as she was checking on the steaks in the broiler, a clean-shaven Wade, wearing off-white jeans and a cream shirt, strode into the kitchen. As usual, the second she felt his presence, her body reacted to him—a reaction she couldn't hide. And Wade knew it.

Without a word, he slid a tape into the portable tape player sitting on the counter and instantly the room was filled with the mellow, late-night sounds of a jazz quartet. The saxophone rose plaintively above the other instruments, and for Kathryn, the music was almost too sensuous, even painful, to listen to.

"D-dinner is ready," she stammered.

"So I see," he murmured somewhere behind her. "Why don't you sit down and I'll take over from here."

Thankful to escape his proximity, she seated herself at the card table. She struggled to present an unconcerned facade while he waited on her and poured her a glass of wine. She felt a curious sense of isolation, sitting in Wade's house in the middle of a meadow as the evening darkened around them.

At the same time she experienced a piercing joy at sharing these precious moments, because they were all she would ever have of him. As she'd prepared dinner, she'd vowed never to be alone with him again. And when Clyde and Alice returned from Canada, she would leave Afton forever.

Since Wade seemed disinclined to talk, they ate their meal in silence. The music should have provided a needed distraction, but she could hardly function, let alone enjoy her food, with Wade seated so close, rarely taking his eyes off her.

Finally she gave up the pretense and excused herself to get a glass of water. But that was a mistake, because while she was standing at the sink, Wade's arms suddenly came around her waist. "Let's dance," he whispered in a husky voice, molding his hands over her hips. The growing insistence of his movements created a sick excitement inside her.

"Please don't do that," she begged feverishly, feeling herself succumb a little more with each caress.

"No one can see us, if that's what you're worried about." He had swept away her long fall of hair and his lips dropped to the heated nape of her neck.

"This is wrong," she cried helplessly, but his touch had weakened her resolve, sapped her will to fight.

"How could it be wrong when we're attracted to each other? I know you're in love with someone else, but I also know your body melts whenever I touch you. It was that way five years ago, and if anything, time seems to have made us more physically attuned than ever. Even though I fought it, I wanted you the moment I saw you at the airport. And you wanted me."

"No!"

"Yes. I could tell by the way you reacted. It isn't something you can hide, Kathryn. You're a sensual woman, yet you seem to be embarrassed by it. You shouldn't be—it's nothing to be ashamed of. In fact, it's a gift the right man would sell his soul to receive."

"But you're not that man." She had to say it and keep on saying it until he believed it! And until *she* did...

At her words, his hands tightened almost painfully around her upper arms. "For tonight I could be. Stay with me. I need you, Kathryn. I need this." His voice shook with emotion as he turned her in his arms and lowered his mouth to hers.

In the early days of their doomed marriage, Philip had kissed her with passion, but nothing in her experience had prepared her for the onslaught of Wade's demands. His kiss, hot with desire, created a longing to love him fully, completely.

But she knew she'd never be satisfied with one night of his lovemaking. She couldn't give in to her needs now, no matter how much she ached for him.

"No, Wade." She managed to sound in control as she wrenched her mouth from his and pushed her hands against his chest. "It's no use."

The finality of her words must have gotten through to him. He didn't try to kiss her again, but she was still locked in his arms.

"Because of him?" Wade demanded bitterly, giving her an angry little shake. Her hair resettled around her shoulders.

Afraid he would discover what she'd been hiding, she averted her face. "Because of many things, not the least of which is the dishonor we would bring to Amy. Do you honestly imagine I could go to bed with you, then calmly meet the woman you're going to marry?"

Her words reverberated in the kitchen as she pulled completely away from him. "And what about Alice and Clyde? My shame would never allow me to look them in the eye again."

A heavy silence pervaded the room. "Where does shame come into it? Answer me that!" he ground out with a ferocity that made her shiver.

Kathryn clung to the sink for support. "We're family, for heaven's sake!" she shouted at him.

"Only in the sense that when my father married Allie, we all came together as a unit. We've been over this ground before. You and I have no blood ties!"

Her face crimsoned. "So that makes it all right for us to carry on a tawdry love affair behind their backs? Behind *Amy's?* I'm amazed you could even consider it!"

He didn't answer right away, but something profound and painful was going on inside him, turning his eyes the dark green of an angry ocean. Unexpectedly he backed away and flipped off the tape player. "If you're ready," he said quietly, "I'll take you home."

She blinked in astonishment; she'd prepared for a battle and then discovered there was none. Bemused by the sudden turn of events and his change in behavior, she followed him silently out of the house to the truck. Something told her he would never again ask her to sleep with him. She should have been thankful that she had finally convinced him. Instead, the knowledge that he would never hold her or kiss her again plunged her into even darker despair.

He didn't try to help her into the cab as he usually did, and this, as much as anything, let her know how completely he was severing all their ties.

However, once they started down the dirt road, he confused her completely by telling her about the rest of his plans for the ranch, conversing in a friendly tone as if that emotion-filled scene in the kitchen had never taken place.

"Next year, when the house is finished, I'm going to build a bunkhouse over there by the cabins to accommodate large groups at one end and store the rafting equipment at the other. When it's completed, the ranch will have a sleeping capacity of fifty."

"I have no doubts it'll be a great success," she answered in a deceptively calm voice. "Who's going to help you run it?"

"My wife, of course, plus a permanent cook and seasonal employees hired as necessary."

Kathryn felt a growing hysteria at the picture of Amy working alongside Wade, and she had no desire to ask more questions.

"I've already mapped out a publicity campaign," he told her. "I'm running ads in papers and magazines back East that cater to families looking for Western vacations. And when things are slow, I have more than enough business as an accountant to keep me afloat."

He flashed her an unfathomable glance. "I'm telling you this so you'll be informed in case anyone wants to know what we've been up to for the the past few hours. And in case Allie wonders why I didn't come in when I dropped you off, you can tell her I haven't seen to the horses yet. Before I go to bed I'll phone the folks to say goodbye.''

For the rest of the drive home, Kathryn stared out her window into the darkness with a grief too deep for tears.

Wade pulled up in front of the house, not bothering to turn into the driveway the way he usually did. "Safe at last," he mocked with a hint of cruelty. "Delivered from a fate worse than...death? Your conscience intact, your body inviolate. Sleep well, *Aunt Kathryn.*"

If he had knocked her down with one of those two-by-fours she'd seen stacked outside his house, he couldn't have caused more pain. She scrambled out of the cab, one part of her desperate to get away from him, the other wanting to throw her arms around his neck and tell him she'd stay with him for as long as he desired her.

Before she had taken two steps, he gunned the accelerator and sped onto the highway. She could only assume he meant to emphasize his intention of leaving her alone in future.

"Was that Wade screeching down the road like a thundering herd was after him?" Clyde didn't sound too pleased as Kathryn entered the dining room where he was folding shirts into a suitcase. Guilt made her wonder if he was upset with her, too.

"He wanted to come in, but he was worried about getting back to feed and water the horses, so he'll phone you in a while."

Clyde shook his head. "I'm afraid there's a lot more bothering Wade than the stock." He eyed her solemnly. "According to Laurel, he asked you over to the ranch this evening. Normally I wouldn't pry, but his behavior lately has been so out of character I wondered if you could enlighten me as to what's going on. You've always had a better rapport with him than any of us."

Not after tonight, Kathryn cried inwardly. "I don't know what to say, Clyde. All he did was show me the ranch and talk about his plans for it."

"Did he mention Amy?"

"No."

Clyde rubbed his neck. "I wish I knew what he was thinking these days."

"Perhaps he's one of those men who gets nervous before their wedding. I understand it's quite normal. Maybe that's what's wrong with Wade." *Maybe it was,* she reasoned to herself, but her own return to Afton had brought on unwanted complications. Her first instincts had been right. The sooner she left Wyoming, the better.

"I'm afraid I can't really understand that, since I wanted to marry your sister from the first moment we met at my store. You were there, clinging to her hand. Remember?"

Kathryn nodded. "But by then you'd already been married—to Wade's mother—and you knew how wonderful it could be." Her voice caught on the last few words. She cleared her throat. "Weren't you the slightest bit nervous before your wedding to her?"

"No," he answered baldly. "We were only nineteen and didn't have the sense to know better, which was a good thing, since we didn't have a great deal of time together before cancer took her. If I'd had Wade's problem, he wouldn't have been born."

Kathryn couldn't respond right away, because despite all the pain, a life that didn't include Wade was incomprehensible to her.

"You're an amazing man, Clyde," she said softly.

"No, just lucky enough to have met two marvelous women who've blessed my life. I wish I could say the same for you. If anyone deserves the very best, it's you."

She blinked back tears. "Not everyone's meant to be married."

He grinned. "Don't you believe it. That's pure propaganda. Everyone needs someone, but not all of us are fortunate enough to meet the right person and be able to do anything about it."

Kathryn turned away, closing her eyes tightly. Clyde couldn't have guessed about her and Wade, or he would never have said what he just did.

She *had* met the right man, but that was where it had to end, for everyone's sake.

"Do me a favor, Clyde, and enjoy your trip with Alice. Getting away will give you a new perspective on all this."

"I think you're right."

Feeling even greater guilt, she rushed to reassure him. "Eventually things will work out for the best. They have to!" She took a deep breath to control her quavering voice. "You and Alice are so lucky to have found each other. Make the most of this time together."

He seemed to ponder her words for a moment, and then a warm smile lighted his face. "We intend to. Thanks for your wise counsel and for being here for the kids." He gave her a quick kiss on the forehead. "By the way, they're planning to help you move into the apartment tomorrow."

"I'm looking forward to it." Impulsively Kathryn threw her arms around Clyde. "I'll never be able to thank you enough for all you've done for me."

"While we're gone, you might think about making Afton your permanent home. This family needs you."

Sadness compounded her guilt. She loved Clyde for saying those words, but Afton could never be her permanent home.

CHAPTER NINE

NORMALLY THE FAMILY walked to work, which was only a half mile down the road from the house. But because they'd gathered for breakfast to see Clyde and Alice off on their trip, Kathryn and the kids were running late and decided to leave for the store in John's car.

Tourists were already lined up outside the front door when he put the key in the lock a few minutes after eight. Customers were in and out all day buying ice, picnic makings, batteries, film and a variety of other supplies. The three of them were kept busy until closing time. After work Kathryn bought her niece and nephew dinner at a nearby diner, and then they started moving her things to the apartment.

The entire process took only half an hour to accomplish. During the move they talked about many things, but on the subject of Wade and Amy, everyone was strangely silent. Kathryn had to admire John for behaving as if nothing was wrong when she knew he was miserable and preoccupied.

It was a relief to finally say good-night. Kathryn rested against the door of her apartment, grateful to be by herself at last. From now on, no matter what pretext brought Wade to the house, she wouldn't be there. They never had to see each other again, not even if he needed supplies from the store. The second she noticed his truck pull into the drive, she'd make an excuse to the others and dash up to her apartment until he left.

Letting out a sigh of disgust at her inability to stop dwelling on him, she hurried into her gleaming new shower and washed her hair. Afterward, she sat down on the blue-and-white-print sofa to write a letter to her best friend, Judy, who was married to an advertising executive and lived in the beach house next to Philip's in San Diego. She was a few years older than Kathryn, with three children. From the beginning the two women had taken to each other, and Judy's support after Kathryn's miscarriage had brought them even closer. Inevitably they shared confidences.

She especially missed her warm caring friend right now and wished she hadn't talked Alice out of installing a phone in the apartment. But it had seemed a waste of money, since Kathryn didn't intend to stay in Afton.

Craving a distraction, she turned on the TV, but without cable there wasn't much to choose from. In truth, nothing could take her mind off Wade. Still, she had to try, so she suffered through a succession of reruns until eleven, when she went to bed.

The next day was a repeat of the first, with customers flocking to the store nonstop. Around four-thirty the phone rang. Since Kathryn was closest she an-

swered it. The caller was Wade, the last person she'd
expected to hear from. Though she'd been rushed off
her feet all day, Wade had never left her thoughts.
Hearing him say her name made her lose all awareness of where she was or what she was doing.

"Y-yes?" She twisted the phone cord around her
fingers. "Did you want to speak to John or Laurel?"

"Not particularly. I'm leaving town in a few minutes and thought I'd better check in with the person in
charge so no one sends out a search party when they
discover I'm away from the ranch."

She assumed he was referring to her accusations a
few days earlier when he couldn't be found and everyone had gone looking for him. He was probably
going to Salt Lake City to be with Amy. She gripped
the receiver a little tighter. "How long will you be
away?"

"As long as it takes."

She hated his condescension. This time she refused
to rise to the bait. "I asked out of concern for your
horses, in case you needed one of us to take care of
them."

"Does that mean you're offering?"

Her face went hot and she turned toward the wall.
"There are customers waiting. If you need help, then
please say so."

"As it happens, I don't."

"Is there anything else?"

"Ask me that question the next time we're alone
and find out."

She was on the verge of telling him there wouldn't be a next time when she heard a click, followed by the dial tone.

Slowly she replaced the receiver. "Aunt Kathryn? What's wrong? Who was on the phone?"

She forgot to fake a smile as she whirled around to face John. "It was Wade. He's leaving town shortly."

"Did he say he was going to Amy's?"

The pain in his voice was real and heart-wrenching. During the past few summers, she'd seen John in various stages of infatuation, but his behavior since she'd come to Afton convinced her he was genuinely in love. Who could have imagined a scenario as twisted and confused as theirs had become?

To ward off an attack of nerves, she started straightening the counter. "No. He only said he'd be away from the ranch for a while and didn't want us to worry when we couldn't find him."

John swore softly. Then he seemed to regain control of himself and waited on a customer needing a fishing license. It was just as well they were too busy to talk, since Kathryn suffered from the same affliction he did. They both wanted someone who could never belong to them, and the torment continued.

Business remained brisk until closing. Once they'd locked up for the night, Cindy came by for Laurel, and John took off in his car. From her apartment window Kathryn watched them go their separate ways, yet all she could think about was Wade. She was almost certain he'd be with Amy tonight and possibly for several other nights, as well. She wondered if they stayed at her house or went off someplace.

Kathryn knew of men who were engaged or married but still had affairs with other women. Somehow Wade didn't fit that picture, and yet wasn't he doing precisely the same thing? Tonight he was with his fiancée, whereas two nights ago he'd been kissing Kathryn and expecting her to spend the night with him at the ranch.

Maybe she should have made love with him. It might have helped get this burning desire for him out of her system. Her longing for him seemed to increase daily, and she couldn't imagine how she'd make it through the rest of her life feeling as she did.

Over the next few days she worked until she was ready to drop. After waiting on customers from eight in the morning until seven in the evening, she spent her nights at the house canning fruit as a welcome-home present for Alice. When Laurel and John offered their help, she declined and told them to go off and do whatever they wanted. Kathryn liked being so exhausted that, when she went back to her apartment, she fell asleep the minute her head touched the pillow. In fact, that was the purpose—to fill every waking moment with activity, to shut out fantasies about Wade.

By Friday she'd finished her canning project and decided to go to bed early, since she and Laurel planned to take a long bike ride the following morning and not report for work until lunchtime. John had suggested they take the whole day off, claiming he had nothing to do but run the store and would manage without them.

Laurel had accepted his offer; she'd already confided to Kathryn that she knew he was missing Amy, which was why he preferred to work long hours. It was a way of coping, as Kathryn knew all too well. Besides, Laurel had always been close to her brother, and Kathryn didn't question her niece's perception.

What did surprise her was Laurel's admission that she and her mother had talked a great deal about John's infatuation with Amy and that they'd concluded it was more serious than first supposed. Secretly Kathryn agreed with that assessment, but refrained from commenting on it. Anxious to change the subject, she'd suggested they get an early start on their bikes the following morning, before the heat became too stifling. Laurel concurred and they arranged to meet in front of the store at seven.

Not long after Kathryn had gone to sleep, something disturbed her. She decided she wasn't yet accustomed to every night sound in her new apartment and tried to go back to sleep. But when she heard knocking followed by a male voice, she quickly sat up in bed.

Since no one could reach her apartment without getting inside the store first, it had to be John. She wondered what would bring him over here this late at night.

She slid out of bed, threw on a robe and hurried into the living room.

The knocking grew louder. "Kathryn? I know you're in there. Open the door."

Her heart tripped over itself. *"Wade?"*

"You sound terrified. I'm sorry if I frightened you, but since you can't be reached by phone, I had no other choice."

"Is something wrong at home?"

"No."

Swallowing hard, she said, "Then couldn't this wait until morning? I'm tired and I have to get up early."

"Let me in, Kathryn, otherwise I'll use my key. Is that what you want?"

The forceful tone of his voice told her he meant it. As soon as she opened the door, he swept past her and shut it again before turning to her with eyes that scorched wherever they touched. He was dressed in a black T-shirt and jeans. He looked so good she had the hysterical desire to throw herself into his arms.

But to remove temptation she did the opposite and backed away from him. "You shouldn't be here, Wade. If someone happens to see your truck outside this time of night, it'll raise all sorts of questions."

He stood there with his hands on his lean hips, as if he was the host and she the intruder. "Very few people know the upstairs of the store is occupied, and in any event, no one would question my right to be here, regardless of the hour."

She cinched the belt of her robe a little tighter. "Why have you come? The last—"

"The last time we were together," he interrupted tersely, "you told me you couldn't let me near you because your conscience wouldn't allow you to make love to an engaged man. Correct me if I'm wrong."

Kathryn made an inarticulate sound in her throat before she managed to speak. "Wade, I don't understand what you're trying to do to me, but I'd like you to leave."

"Why?" he asked, taking a step toward her. "Why should I? There's no reason for me to go. I'm no longer engaged to Amy."

"What?" The room started to tip crazily.

"You heard me. It's the reason I went to Salt Lake, to break it off with her. If you don't believe me, call the house. John will verify it, because I've just come from there. I've explained to him that Amy and I are through and that I'm reasonably certain she wants comforting from him.

Kathryn shook her head. "I don't believe it."

His eyes narrowed on her face. "What don't you believe? It's very simple really. What you said in the tent was true. Amy isn't the great love of my life. She never was and never could be, wonderful though she is."

"Wade," she wailed, "I had no right to say anything that night!"

"Why not? I should never have gotten engaged to her in the first place."

They stared hard at each other. "Why did you?" she asked before she could stop herself.

"She didn't like the fact that my work kept us apart so much of the time, and I foolishly believed a ring might make her feel more secure. What happened was that she spent every available moment since the end of May in Afton—with John—waiting around for me."

So that was how John and Amy had become so close. "Is that the only reason you got engaged?" She dreaded the answer.

"No." After a brief pause he said, "I decided to make that much of a commitment to find out if what I felt for her could last a lifetime." His mouth twisted in self-deprecation. "Obviously it couldn't last one day after you came back into my life."

"I'm not in your life, Wade."

"I don't know what else you'd call it."

She couldn't take much more of this. "You know better than anyone that Alice begged me to come for a visit. Against my better judgment, I accepted her invitation. She's the reason I'm here. The only reason."

As she spoke, his face changed, growing still and pale. "If there's one thing to be salvaged from all this," she went on, "it's that you discovered how you felt about Amy before it was too late. I'd hate to see anyone go through what I—" She suddenly broke off, aware that she was giving away far too much.

"Why stop now?" he goaded. "Are you afraid to admit that marrying Lawson for his money wasn't enough? That you had to turn to another man for...love?"

Heat flooded her cheeks. "Did Clyde tell you that?"

A strange smile lifted one corner of his mouth. "He didn't need to. Your response said it all. But that was never our problem, was it, Kathryn?"

Horrified that he was so close to the truth, she said, "It may surprise you to know that I've kissed other men, *older* men—" she paused "—with even greater pleasure."

It hurt Kathryn deeply to say such cruel things to him, but she forced herself to continue. "Maybe that's *your* problem Wade. You haven't had enough experience yet. Now that you're not engaged, I suggest you acquire some, so you'll know the real thing when it comes along."

"I intend to," he murmured in a husky voice, ignoring her sarcasm. "And frankly, on the way back from Salt Lake, the only thing I had on my mind was this." In the next instant he pulled her into his arms and found her mouth with his own.

Each time they came together after a separation, his kisses managed to break down her resistance a little more. The rapture he created with his lips, his body, drove her to respond with the same overpowering urgency.

Until she remembered it was wrong. Then she fought him as if her life depended on it.

He backed her against the wall, "I'm free of entanglements and so are you. What's going on, Kathryn?" His chest rose and fell with heightened emotion.

She didn't want to look at him, but his hand easily spanned her throat, checking her movements. "I—I admit I'm attracted to you physically, but if you think I'm going to indulge myself behind the family's back, you don't know me at all!"

Wade's eyes burned into hers. "Then it's time they understood how it is between us. No more games." Before she could protest, he lowered his head and once again she was lost in the consuming fire of his kiss. "It's five years too late for pretence," he murmured against her lips. "I made a rash decision when I got engaged. It was all an effort to fight my feelings for you, but it backfired. Now I want to be open about the two of us and—"

"No, Wade!" she half sobbed. Tears of fright ran down her cheeks.

But he remained unmoved. "Do you honestly think it's going to come as any great surprise to the family? They've seen us together. There's no doubt they've felt the chemistry between us." He drew her resisting hand to his heart and held it there.

"Feel that!" he whispered fiercely. "Whenever you're around it pounds like a war drum." Before she could protest, his free hand slid over her heart. "Yours is hammering even faster. And the pulse at your throat, it dances against my lips when I kiss you like this."

She moaned in ecstasy as his questing mouth grazed her neck and throat, finding that certain sensitive spot.

"Do you have any idea how rare it is for two people to respond to each other as we do, Kathryn?"

Summoning all her strength, she squeezed past him and positioned herself behind one of the living-room chairs. "However true that may be, I refuse to do anything about it. And if you say one word to Clyde and Alice, you'll hurt them—you'll destroy this family—for no good reason. Because I'm leaving for Colorado as soon as they return and I won't be coming back."

"Don't you mean California?" he asked violently. "What happened? Did he call you and tell you he's divorcing his wife, after all?"

"No," she stated with a finality that formed grim brackets around his mouth. "I told you in the tent. That period of my life is over and I have no intention of seeing him or fantasizing about him again. Right now, my only priority is to get on with my career and find a permanent place to live."

"What do you call this apartment?" he demanded. "You can teach here in Afton."

"But that isn't what I want."

His features hardened. "So what are you saying? That despite the desire you feel for me, you'd rather be someplace else?"

She avoided his gaze, haunted by the undertone of pain she could hear in his voice. "That's right. Do you think I make a practice of going to bed with any man I find myself attracted to because I can't have the man I love?"

"I don't know the answer to that, do I? You went as far as to marry Philip without really loving him. What was that all about?"

She backed farther away. "It-it's time for you to go."

Too late she saw the rage that swept through him, and before she could think, he clutched her upper arms and dragged her against him. His kiss could have been a brand, the way its blue-hot fire burned through to her soul. When he finally put her away from him, she staggered backward.

"If you really believe you're going to find answers in Colorado, then you're not the woman I thought you were. Dear Lord, how could I have been so wrong?" He pivoted and strode out.

The apartment door banged shut, enclosing her in deadly silence. Scalding tears poured down her cheeks. She wanted to call him back, beg him to stay. She'd hurt his pride, just as she had five years ago, but this time there was one major difference. He was a man now, and in her heart she knew he'd never come back.

That knowledge cut like a knife, deepening an old wound that would never heal. She sat on the couch for the rest of the night, trying to imagine Clyde and Alice's reaction if they knew how strongly she and Wade were attracted to each other.

Clyde was an extremely moral, principled man who adored his children. And Kathryn suspected that his feelings for Wade had a depth, an intensity that exceeded even his loving relationships with John and

Laurel. For several years after his first wife's death, he and Wade had clung to each other, and soul-deep bonds were forged between them—bonds that made Clyde exceptionally protective of his oldest son.

When Alice met Clyde, she'd loved him and Wade immediately, but throughout the years, Kathryn noticed how very careful her sister had been not to overstep her bounds where their father-son relationship was concerned. As a result, Kathryn had an idea Alice put Wade on a pedestal without even being aware of it.

What would happen to the harmony in this family if it was suddenly discovered that Wade and Kathryn had succumbed to their mutual attraction? And what would be the point of Alice and Clyde's knowing, anyway, since all Wade seemed to want was an affair? How long could it possibly last? Kathryn didn't want that type of relationship—and certainly not with him.

She had no doubt Clyde would be shocked and bitterly disappointed. Just telling him the truth would raise questions in his mind about everything that had gone on in the past. He would lose his trust in Kathryn, and in his own son. The situation would become sordid and ugly. She couldn't bear that, couldn't bear the thought of a breach developing between him and Wade.

As for Alice, Kathryn knew her sister's first loyalty was to her husband, where it belonged. After driving a wedge into the family, Kathryn would no longer be welcome in their home, and relationships would be shattered forever.

The situation had reached an impasse. From now on, Kathryn would be counting the hours till Clyde and Alice came back from their trip. As soon as they arrived she would take the bus from Afton to Boulder. After buying a new car, she'd find herself a condo in the nice residential area where she had lived before and seek a temporary teaching job until a position at the university opened up. Her sole commitment would be to her career.

Though she dreaded contact with the family, Kathryn planned to keep her date with Laurel, and when her niece arrived the next morning she was ready. Laurel would know about Wade's broken engagement and she'd naturally want to talk about it. That was what Kathryn dreaded most as she walked out the front door of the store to greet her.

But her fears took a different turn when she noticed Laurel was dressed for work rather than biking.

"Before you say anything, I have something important to tell you!" the girl exclaimed excitedly.

"What is it?" Kathryn tried to sound properly interested without giving herself away.

"Last night Wade showed up at the house and told me and John that he's no longer engaged to Amy. Apparently they talked things over and decided it would be best to call it off. Permanently!" A brilliant smile lit up Laurel's face. "I knew he didn't love her. I knew it!"

"And what about Amy?" Kathryn inserted quietly.

"Wade said she was as relieved as he was. He said that for the past month, he'd been aware Amy's feelings had changed. When he confronted her, she admitted she was confused and thought maybe she'd better give the ring back. And we know why, don't we?" Laurel looked delighted.

Kathryn's lips curved in a half smile. "Do we?"

"Of course we do! It's because she loves John and John loves her. You should have seen John's face when Wade told us the news. John tried not to react but, Aunt Kathryn, I watched him and it was like seeing somebody dead come back to life!"

Kathryn could understand that. "And Wade? How do you think he's taking it?"

She eyed Kathryn steadily, then shrugged. "Like Wade takes everything. In his stride. I don't feel sorry for him, because he was never in love with her in the first place. He proved it when he said he purposely didn't invite Amy on our camping trip. He admitted that he preferred being alone with the family. He said that's when he knew he couldn't go on the way things were."

At Laurel's words, the pounding of Kathryn's heart became almost painful.

"Wade's a deep one," Laurel observed, staring at Kathryn intently. "But someday, when he finds the right woman, we'll all know about it and there'll be no doubts. I can't wait till Mom and Dad get home to tell them the news!''

Kathryn cleared her throat. ''And how do you think they'll feel?''

''Overjoyed. They love Amy. We all do. She and John are perfect together. And that's what I have to talk to you about. John's going to drive down to Salt Lake and see her today. He might be gone for a couple of days, so we'll have to run the store without his help. Is that okay with you?''

Kathryn's head swam to think the situation could turn around so dramatically in just a few hours. ''Of course. We can go for a ride after work if you want.''

''Great. I'll go put my bike in the back room.''

''Have you had breakfast yet?''

''No, but I was hoping you'd ask.''

''Then come up to the apartment and I'll fix some toast and juice.''

''We're going to need it, especially with the Saturday herd.''

Actually Kathryn was glad they were in for a heavy day. She didn't want time to think about anything— such as driving over to the ranch and hurling herself into Wade's arms. Right now her resistance to him was so low that if he walked through the front door and called her name, she'd follow him anywhere. And she'd stay with him, for as long as he wanted her.

CHAPTER TEN

ON SATURDAY NIGHT, after they'd locked up the store, Laurel begged Kathryn to go home with her to spend the night. They were both too tired to go cycling, so making pizza and watching a horror movie together seemed an ideal alternative. Though Kathryn wanted to be alone, she didn't dare disappoint her niece, not when everyone else was away, including Cindy.

The evening was uneventful, and Kathryn, who could hardly keep her cyes open, went to bed in Wade's old room. Laurel stayed up to watch the late show and answer Steve Newton's latest letter. If Kathryn hadn't been afraid that Wade might walk in on them, she would have had a cup of coffee and kept Laurel company. But she couldn't risk another confrontation, not when she was feeling so vulnerable.

On Sunday morning they slept in, had a late breakfast and went to church. Afterward Laurel suggested they go for their postponed bike ride. Even though it was hot, Kathryn agreed; it meant being away from the house—and from any chance encounters with Wade. After an hour, however, they both found the heat too oppressive and headed back for a cool shower.

"Mom and Dad are home!"

Kathryn looked in the direction of the house. Sure enough, Clyde's Dodge was parked in the driveway. Relief swept over her. Now that they'd returned from their trip, she could make arrangements to leave Afton.

Clyde must have heard Laurel's excited cry, because he opened the back door and rushed out to kiss them both when they'd dismounted their bikes. For the next few minutes there was the usual commotion, with everyone hugging and trying to talk at once. Alice, unable to get over the fact that Kathryn had canned all her peaches and pears while they'd been away, thanked her profusely.

They finally moved into the house so Kathryn and Laurel could quench their thirst. Kathryn didn't miss the private message Alice flashed Clyde when Laurel told her parents to sit down, saying she had an important announcement.

They did, and Laurel proceeded to explain. It appeared she'd been right when she said her parents would be pleased by the news. In fact, Clyde was beaming as he asked Laurel to take a drive to the service station and keep her "old dad company."

After they'd gone, Alice sat there staring at Kathryn; for once, Kathryn had no idea what her sister was thinking. To hide her nervousness she went over to the sink for another glass of water.

"Clyde and I decided to drop by the ranch and see Wade on our way to Afton, but he wasn't home. When we went into his study, where he always leaves his messages, we discovered one waiting for us." Kathryn's head jerked up. "It said he'd broken his engagement to Amy and would give us the details after he got back from California."

"California?" Kathryn said in bewilderment.

Alice went on, "He also said that if we couldn't wait for an explanation until he came back, we were to ask *you* what happened the other night, when the two of you were together at the apartment."

Kathryn wanted to crawl into a hole and die. She stood there in silence, the hand holding the glass of water visibly trembling.

"Actually, I don't think I *can* wait," Alice asserted, "so why don't you tell me what's going on?"

An uncomfortable heat enveloped Kathryn, and she found herself at a total loss for words.

"You know the real reason for his breakup with Amy, don't you?"

Kathryn's heart thudded too fast. "I have some idea, yes."

"You look a little ill. Sit down, honey." Kathryn sank into the nearest chair and drained her glass of water. For a few minutes neither of them said anything as Alice studied her younger sister. Kathryn recognized that look and shuddered. "Why don't we start at the beginning," Alice suggested quietly.

"Beginning?" Her voice came out as a squeak. Right this minute she couldn't think. Not when she was afraid Wade had taken it into his head to have a talk with Philip. Why else would he go there? How dared he?

"Ever since you arrived from San Diego, Wade has become an entirely different person. Obviously something significant is going on. Won't you tell me what it is?"

If Alice had been angry or demanding, Kathryn might have excused herself and left the house without saying a word. But her sister's gentle voice, her compassionate demeanor, made it impossible for Kathryn to ignore her entreaty.

"What exactly did Wade's note say?" she asked.

"Just that you'd tell us why he broke his engagement."

"That's all?"

Alice nodded slowly.

Kathryn buried her face in her hands, barely able to believe Wade had done this to her. Angry at her rejection, he had placed her in an untenable position with the family, compelling her to reveal the very things she had intended to keep secret for the rest of her life.

If he had any idea what he'd done, he obviously didn't care. She would never forgive him for this treachery.

"I know we've had a conversation about this before," Alice said, "but I'm going to ask you again. What happened between the two of you the summer Clyde and I took the kids to Banff? When we came home, you were gone, and Wade had changed beyond recognition. He's never been the same since. For that matter, neither have you. Did he do something to hurt you and you're protecting him? I swear it won't go any further than these walls. You're my little sister. I love you. And though I love Wade, if his behavior has kept you away from us all this time, I have to know the truth. This simply can't go on any longer."

"He's never hurt me," she whispered. *Except now,* her heart cried out.

Alice blinked. "Has he pressured you, then? I've always known he preferred your company to anyone else's and worried that he was demanding too much of your time. In fact, we planned that trip to Canada five years ago to coincide with Wade's trip to Yosemite, so you could have the house to yourself for a few days. Clyde and I received one of the biggest shocks of our lives when we learned that at the last minute he'd canceled with his friends and stayed home with you. I have no doubt he did it on purpose. John and Laurel *know* he did."

Kathryn took a fortifying breath. "I have to admit I was surprised when he came back to the house later that day."

"Did you fight over it?"

"No." *Anything but.*

After a pause Alice said, "Were you glad when he showed up?"

"What?" Kathryn was on her feet in an instant, almost knocking over the chair.

Instead of the dreaded anger she'd feared, Kathryn saw only warmth and compassion shining from Alice's blue eyes. "You know what I'm asking," her sister answered patiently.

Kathryn turned away. "I'm very fond of Wade. You know that."

"That's an interesting word," Alice observed dryly. "However, two people don't undergo drastic changes in behavior and personality because they're *fond* of each other. Kathryn," she said in a calm, sweet voice, "are you embarrassed to admit you're attracted to Wade? Is that what this is all about?"

Kathryn's defenses crumbled. First her shoulders shook and then she broke down sobbing. The minute Alice's arms went around her, she cried harder, needing release from the storm raging inside her.

"Do you think I'm terrible, Alice? Do you hate me? Please don't hate me," she begged her sister. "I never meant for it to happen. Neither of us did."

"Kathryn Barker Lawson," Alice said sternly, shaking her gently by the shoulders. "Where on earth did you get the idea I could ever hate you for anything? Let alone for falling in love with Wade?"

Hearing those words, Kathryn felt herself go weak. "How long have you known?" The words were a jerky whisper.

Alice cocked one delicate eyebrow. "I think when you asked me if Amy would make Wade a good wife. There was a longing, a wistfulness, in your voice that gave you away."

She shook her head. "All this time you've known." Her heart hammered painfully. "Does Clyde suspect?" she asked, her eyes shimmering with tears.

"Yes. He saw it in a dozen different ways while we were in the Tetons. But it was John and Laurel who guessed before either of us. They both said that Wade's always been so crazy about you no other woman had a prayer. And whenever you're with Wade, no one else exists for you."

"I can't believe what I'm hearing," Kathryn moaned.

"Why? It's perfectly understandable. You and Wade have no blood tie and you were thrown together from the beginning. That created a real closeness, a bond of understanding between you. Besides, I have eyes in my head and I can see Wade's a heartbreaker just like his father."

"But I'm five years older than he is." Kathryn was still having difficulty taking it all in.

"Age doesn't mean anything when you get older. You know that. And Wade was always more mature than his friends. Probably because he and Clyde had to go through so much together. What amazes me is that Wade's the only person in this family who doesn't know you're in love with him. That's why your marriage didn't work, isn't it?"

"Yes," Kathryn admitted quietly.

"Were you and Wade...intimate before you left for San Diego? You don't have to answer that if you don't want to."

"No, I mean yes. I mean—no, we weren't, but yes, we came close. I was so frightened, so appalled at my own behavior, I couldn't leave Afton fast enough."

Alice let out a heavy sigh. "Finally it all fits. When I read the letter telling us about your marriage aloud, Wade went white as a sheet. He didn't say a word to anybody. The next thing we knew he'd packed his camping gear and taken off for the Tetons. He was gone a week. When he did come back, he'd turned into a stranger and couldn't seem to get along with anybody. The next thing we knew, he announced he was leaving to attend Colorado State."

"I had no idea."

"That was not the best year for the Matheson family. You cheated me out of a big wedding, and Clyde went around here as grouchy as a bear. And that's not like my husband."

"No." Kathryn began crying again. "I'm so sorry for all the pain I . . . we caused everybody."

"Stop apologizing for something that happened naturally and was probably inevitable from the beginning."

"All right," Kathryn murmured, wiping her eyes.

"Now, answer me one final question. Why did Wade take off for California?"

"I—I'm not sure."

"Oh, I think you are. Might as well tell me everything, since I'm going to find out, anyway."

Rubbing her palms against her knees, Kathryn said, "When Wade picked me up at the airport, I realized the desire I felt for him was stronger than ever. But I also knew he was engaged. To fight the attraction, I purposely led him to believe I'm in love with another man, to explain why my marriage to Philip didn't work. It's been safer that way. The other night when he came to the apartment and told me he'd broken off with Amy, I'm afraid I made matters worse."

"How much worse?" Alice prodded.

Kathryn hesitated only a moment before revealing everything that had happened.

Alice was slow to respond. "I'd say you've broken his heart a second time."

"His heart?"

"Now that I know the truth, I'm going to let you in on a little secret. It's something I withheld from you that evening we were sitting in front of our tent at the lake."

"What?"

Alice's mouth curved into her warm lovely smile. "When I first told Wade you were coming to Afton for a vacation, he didn't say a word. But I saw the light explode in his eyes like...like hot green sparks. It told me everything. That was the look missing with Amy. That's the look I want to see in his eyes permanently. And apparently you're the only woman who can put it there."

"Alice? Are you saying what I think you're saying?"

Her sister's eyes narrowed provocatively. "If I were you, I'd be at that ranch waiting for Wade when he gets back. You've hurt him, honey. You've hurt him so badly it's going to take a lot of convincing to bring him around. But you have the most important thing of all in your favor."

Kathryn's throat was so choked with emotion, she could hardly speak. "What's that?"

"He's in love with you, too. I think he always has been. Do I need to add that Clyde and I couldn't be happier?"

Kathryn grabbed Alice's hands, squeezing them convulsively. "Are you being honest with me? Clyde doesn't hate me?"

"Honey—" she leaned forward and smoothed the hair from Kathryn's brow "—Clyde loves you, and now that he knows his son loves you, he can hardly wait for the two of you to get things resolved, so we can go back to being a contented family again."

Kathryn shook her head. "I still can't believe it. All this time I've been so terrified of him finding out and... and disapproving."

Alice chuckled. "I guess I'm going to have to let you in on one more secret." At Kathryn's puzzled expression she said, "It's the last, I promise. You know whose idea it was to go to Banff this time, don't you?"

"Yes. It was Clyde's, because he wanted to take you on a second honeymoon."

"Not exactly. Yes, it *was* Clyde's idea. But didn't you find it odd he would want to take a trip like this when you'd barely arrived from California and hadn't been with us for more than a few days?"

"To be honest, I never thought about it."

"That's because your love for Wade has made you oblivious to a lot of things. I'm going to tell you something that'll put you at peace about Clyde's feelings. He had this idea that if we left and went on vacation, like we did five years ago, it would give you and Wade, and ultimately John and Amy, a chance to work out your problems. He figured if he said it was a second honeymoon, you wouldn't turn us down when we asked you to work at the store and be around for John and Laurel."

"You're kidding, aren't you? *That's* why you left?"

Alice nodded. "The only reason. And his plan worked!" She leaned over again and hugged her younger sister. "We have a second honeymoon every time we travel. And though we loved Banff, it wasn't our best trip, considering we decided not to phone home. Instead, we had to worry and speculate and wonder how things were going—and pray for a miracle. Kathryn, when we read Wade's message, Clyde let out a whoop of delight you could hear from Afton to the Tetons. Does that answer your question?"

ON THE THIRD NIGHT of her vigil at the ranch, Kathryn finally saw the headlights of a car approaching the house. From where she stood at the kitchen window, she couldn't distinguish the make. But it had to be either a family member or Wade, since no one else could get past the main gate.

Though she'd gone over this moment in her mind a hundred times or more, she still didn't know exactly what she was going to say. Everything depended on Wade's reaction.

She had taken pains to make herself look as attractive as possible, wearing her shiny brown hair loose and flowing from a side part. The black-on-white cotton print dress with its dropped waist and cap sleeves was one Wade had never seen before, and it flattered her slender figure. To complete her outfit, she wore white sandals and gold hoop earrings.

The sound of the engine grew louder. She could finally see the white truck, revealed by the lights from the front porch. Hectic color filled her cheeks, and her heart began to jump erratically from sheer nervousness. She hurried to the front foyer and stood waiting.

The slam of the truck door made her start. Then she heard footsteps on the porch and the sound of a key being inserted into the lock.

Kathryn held her breath, amazed at her own temerity in coming to Wade like this. Always in the past he had come to her.

Would he tell her to get out? Would he give her a chance to explain anything? She had no idea, but she was growing more frightened by the second and felt nervous perspiration bead her brow.

He stormed into the house as if pursued and closed the door so hard the house shook. Because his head was bent, he didn't immediately see her standing off to the side. At the sight of him, her mouth went dry, and it became difficult to form any sound at all.

When he headed directly for the living-room area, she softly called his name. He wheeled around in surprise, then sucked in his breath when he saw her. She noted the lines around his mouth. His shirt was limp and creased, his face gaunt with exhaustion.

For the longest time he didn't say anything. His lids drooped as he appraised her coldly, and she couldn't imagine his eyes alive with light, the way Alice had described.

"You're supposed to be in Colorado. What are you doing here?" he said at last.

"I couldn't leave—because of what you wrote in the note to Clyde and Alice."

His bitter smile devastated her. "That must have been an interesting experience. I wonder what lies you told them this time."

She lifted her head and spoke quietly. "For once I told the truth. The whole truth."

"Which truth is that?"

"Wade—" She started to answer but he cut her off.

"I had an interesting chat with an old friend of yours this morning. When I couldn't find your ex-husband at the university, I drove to your famous beach house. Your friendly neighbor, Judy, informed me he was out of the country. But she was willing to fill me in on a few facts when she found out we're family. Namely, that your marriage failed because you were in love with someone here in Wyoming."

"That's true." She didn't blink an eyelash.

Obviously he hadn't been expecting her capitulation; his head flew back in obvious shock. "You purposely led me to believe it was someone you met in California."

"No, I didn't. You assumed as much, and I decided to let you think what you wanted because... because it seemed the best way to handle things at the time."

"Who's the man, Kathryn? I know every man you ever knew or had a relationship with."

Swallowing hard, she said, "Actually, you're better acquainted with him than anyone else in the world."

A minute passed without a word from him, but his face had gone a sickly gray color and she saw him stagger under the weight of some terrible burden. "Dear Lord, you're in love with Dad. How have I been so blind?"

Something between a laugh and a cry burst from her throat. "No, Wade, darling!" She ran to him and threw her arms around his neck, but he pushed her away with so much force she almost fell.

"Everything's beginning to make sense. All this time you've been in love with your sister's husband. At the lake, you were gone so long bringing him back to camp, everyone wondered why." He groaned with a pain she could feel in her heart. "Did you tolerate my kisses because I look like him?" He breathed heavily, painfully. "I suppose I have to give you credit for putting me off..."

He bolted for the front door, but Kathryn had anticipated his movements and blocked his exit. "You're not leaving this house until we get something straight. I'm in love with *you*, Wade Matheson. It's always been you, from the very beginning."

"Get out of my way!"

Horrified that he wouldn't believe her, she reacted instinctively and grasped his face with both hands. "*I love you.* Why else do you think I'd be here waiting for you?" she cried.

When she pressed her warm ardent mouth to his, he didn't respond. His body remained hard and unyielding, but she refused to let him go. She melted against him, trying with her whole being and with every movement of her body to show him that he was her life.

Kathryn had never taken the initiative in lovemaking. Not with Philip, because she'd never felt enough desire. And not with Wade, because she'd always been afraid it would flare out of control. But everything was different now. She was free to express her love. She slid her hands inside his shirt to caress his chest while her mouth covered his face with kisses.

Slowly, inexorably, she felt his tension give way, and that tiny bit of success made her bolder. She kissed his ear, his neck, then moved the collar of his shirt aside so she could taste the skin of his shoulder. "I love you, Wade. So much you can't possibly imagine. Don't go away now, not when I've been waiting three days," she begged feverishly. "I've been waiting for you, wanting you, until I thought I'd lose my mind."

A hoarse cry escaped his throat. Suddenly he began kissing her, savagely at first, as if he couldn't quite believe she was real. Then he seemed to finally understand that her own kisses were given without reservation. The pressure of his mouth changed, became so exquisite, so loving, she almost reeled from the pleasure.

"Wade," she gasped, "hold me. Don't ever let me go." She kissed his mouth passionately. "I've wanted this for five long miserable years."

"I've wanted it longer," he confessed. On a low groan, he picked her up in his arms. Dizzy with sensation, she clung to him, continuing their kiss as he carried her through the house to his bedroom. When the phone rang, she broke away to whisper, "I'm sure that's Alice. She's been calling periodically to find out if you were home yet. If I don't answer, she'll probably come over."

"Then answer it." Still holding her against his heart, he lowered himself to the bed.

With an unsteady hand she reached for the phone propped on the beside table. "H-hello?" she said shakily.

"Kathryn?" It was Clyde. "You sound upset. Do you want us to come over?"

"No. Clyde? Wade's back," was all she could get out before Wade said into the phone, "Hi, Dad. You can relax now." As he spoke, his eyes traveled over her face. They were alive with color, just as Alice had said, filling Kathryn with the greatest happiness she'd ever experienced.

"Kathryn and I have wedding plans to make. We'll tell you about them in the morning. Right now we have five years of catching up to do."

Suddenly Kathryn could hear Alice's voice. "Since you two have waited this long, why not come home and spend the night with us?"

Wade's chuckle grew into full-blown laughter. Still smiling, he lowered his mouth to give Kathryn a deep hard kiss. "Obviously," he said to her, "they don't like the idea of us spending the night alone at the ranch."

Kathryn's expression must have revealed her disappointment, because Wade murmured in her ear, sending a delicious thrill through her body. "I don't want to go to their house, either. I'm leaving this decision entirely up to you." He tugged playfully on her earlobe for emphasis.

She traced his mouth with her index finger. "I'm so thankful they're on our side. I don't want to do anything to upset them now," she said softly, kissing the places she had touched. They gazed into each other's eyes, a gaze of perfect understanding, before Wade spoke into the phone again.

"You drive a hard bargain, Allie. Where am I supposed to sleep? I'm warning you right now, I'm not letting Kathryn out of my sight."

"On the couch, of course."

Wade's bark of laughter made Kathryn smile.

"All right," he finally agreed. "We'll be over in a while. But don't hold your breath." Then he handed the phone to Kathryn. "Dad wants to speak to you," he whispered.

"Clyde?"

"Honey, in case you two don't make it over here tonight, I just wanted to tell you how happy we are about this."

Everything she needed to hear was in his voice—his love, his approval, his acceptance. "Oh, Clyde," she barely managed to say before the tears began.

"Hang up the phone, Kathryn," Wade ordered loudly enough for his parents to hear, his face transformed by a deep frown. When she did, he demanded, "What's wrong?"

"Nothing's *wrong*," she hastened to assure him. "Just the apposite. Your father gave me his blessing and now everything's so right!"

With those words she was once again lost in the wonder of his kiss. Time and place were forgotten as the passion that had been smoldering in both of them burst into uncontrollable flame.

"It's no use," Wade whispered in a husky voice. He reluctantly let her go, forcing himself off the bed. "I can't touch you without wanting to keep you in bed all night. Let's go to the house and get it over with. But I want you to know that I'm not waiting any longer than necessary to get married."

"I don't want to wait, either." Trembling with desire, she got to her feet and had to brace herself against the bed to stand.

"I know they'd like us to have a big church wedding and invite everyone in Star Valley. But that'll take several weeks to organize."

"You're right."

"So tonight let's talk to them while you pack. My cases are already in the truck. We can drive to Salt Lake and catch a plane for Reno. We'll be married as soon as we get there, then honeymoon in Tahoe. Nobody will have to know except the family. While we're gone, they can make wedding plans to their hearts' content."

Dazed by the turn of events, she could only nod in agreement. She followed him from the room and, as he locked up the house, watched his every action with longing in her eyes.

Before they walked out the front door, he reached for her and pulled her into his arms. "In my heart, I built this house for us. Little did I dream you'd end up living here with me."

She raised solemn eyes to his. "I hope you won't regret it fifty years from now."

He tenderly kissed each eyelid closed, then pressed a hot kiss on her avid mouth. "From the very beginning I've loved you, wanted to be around you all the time. Those feelings have only deepened, and they'll keep getting stronger as we go through the rest of our lives together. I've always known we were meant for each other, Kathryn."

"I'm convinced of it," she said, her voice shaking. "Otherwise I'd still be married to Philip. I tried to make him a good wife, but you were there in my heart, and Philip knew it."

Wade's face sobered. "At least now he and Amy are free to find the person who'll love them as they deserve to be loved," he said gently. "But forgive me if I have no regrets about *our* love. It eventually brought you back where you belong."

"Oh, Wade." She slid her arms around his waist, burying her moist face against his neck. "When you came to the apartment the other night, I didn't mean to hurt you. The last thing I wanted was to be cruel, but I was so afraid of Clyde and Alice's reaction."

"I know." He tangled his hand in her silky hair. "It's something I've never been able to understand. They're rational people, darling. In order to prove that to you, I decided to put you in a position you couldn't squirm your way out of."

She couldn't resist a tiny laugh and lifted her flushed face to look at him. "You did that all right."

"Apparently it worked," he teased, kissing the end of her nose.

"You know Alice too well. She came after me full throttle. I didn't stand a chance."

"And in the process, you found out your fears were all for nothing."

She kissed him over and over again. "I still can't believe it. Alice actually sounded happy about us."

"Why does that surprise you? They know we've always been crazy about each other. Now they'll have us around forever and be able to watch our children grow up."

"So many times I've dreamed about being pregnant with your baby," she whispered haltingly.

"Babies," he corrected as he brushed his mouth against hers. "I want a houseful. Am I rushing you?"

"No, darling. We don't have time to wait. I'm—"

He silenced her with a long lingering kiss. "I never again want to hear you tell me how old you are. Believe me, it's indelibly impressed on my mind."

"I promise," she said when he released her.

"Good. Then let's get out of here so we can get started on our lives together." He sent her a loving look, and she was filled with warmth.

A few minutes later the ranch gate closed behind the truck. Kathryn snuggled against Wade and pressed her lips to the side of his neck and throat. He returned her kiss, then murmured, "I suppose you're aware that our news is going to make John ecstatic. If he and Amy discover they're truly in love, they'll eventually be able to make plans without feeling any guilt or embarrassment."

"I know, and the sense of relief I'm feeling is almost as great as the joy."

Wade shook his head in wonder. "I drove in here a while ago, so low, so depressed, I didn't see the point to my life anymore. When you called my name from the front hall, I swear I thought I was hallucinating."

She smoothed the hair from his brow. "I've been at the ranch for three days, waiting..."

"Three days," he repeated. "Three more days we've wasted." He clasped her hand and held on to it. "But never again."

Her heart chanted those words as they drove onto the flower-lined highway. Her long exile was over. She had finally come home.

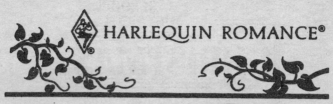

HARLEQUIN ROMANCE®

Valerie Bloomfield comes home to Orchard Valley, Oregon, for the saddest of reasons. Her father has suffered a serious heart attack, and now his three daughters are gathering at his side, praying he'll survive.

Orchard Valley

This visit home will change Valerie's life—especially when she meets Colby Winston, her father's handsome and strong-willed doctor!

"The Orchard Valley trilogy features three delightful, spirited sisters and a trio of equally fascinating men. The stories are rich with the romance, warmth of heart and humor readers expect, and invariably receive, from Debbie Macomber."

—Linda Lael Miller

Don't miss the Orchard Valley trilogy by Debbie Macomber:

VALERIE Harlequin Romance #3232 (November 1992)
STEPHANIE Harlequin Romance #3239 (December 1992)
NORAH Harlequin Romance #3244 (January 1993)

Look for the special cover flash on each book!

Available wherever Harlequin books are sold   ORC-G